Molly's Fire

Janet Lee Carey

Molly's Fire

ATHENEUM BOOKS *for* YOUNG READERS

NEW YORK   LONDON   TORONTO   SYDNEY   SINGAPORE

Atheneum Books for Young Readers
An imprint of Simon & Schuster Children's Publishing Division
1230 Avenue of the Americas
New York, New York 10020
Copyright © 2000 by Janet Lee Carey
Book design by Angela Carlino
The text of this book is set in Janson Text.
Printed in the United States of America
2 4 6 8 10 9 7 5 3 1
Library of Congress Cataloging-in-Publication Data
Carey, Janet Lee.
Molly's fire / by Janet Lee Carey.
p. cm.
Summary: Back home in Maine, Molly refuses to believe the
telegram that says her pilot father is presumed dead when his
plane is shot down in Holland during World War II.
ISBN 0-689-82612-5
[1. Fathers and daughters—Fiction. 2. World War, 1939-
1945—Fiction. 3. Maine—Fiction.] I. Title.
PZ7.C2125 Mo 2000
[Fic]—dc21   99-47058

For my parents, Margaret Saxby and Truman Lee. For my husband, Thomas, and friend Cynthia Finney. With special thanks to Jonathan J. Lanman, Jean E. Karl, and my agent, Irene W. Kraas.

For those who lost their lives in World War II, and for those who were left behind.

Beloved, think it not strange concerning the fiery trial which is to try you, . . .

l Peter 4:12

one

St. George's Ruin

Molly raced down Keenan Beach, dodging driftwood limbs that were scattered like giant bones along the shore. Waves swept up the Maine coast. They tumbled in and pulled away, leaving ribbon kelp and seashells entangled in the driftwood branches. Molly sped up. The salt wind slapped her cheeks and blew back her red hair as she ran. Find Kevin, that's all she had to do, then she'd be free to climb the trail to St. George's Ruin and dig up the rest of the stained glass. She'd wanted to go to the ruin all week, but Mom's never-ending list of chores had kept her away.

Leaping over a dead crab, she stopped to catch her breath and scanned the climbing rocks ahead. Down the cove, Kevin's blond head appeared as he crested a boulder. He stood on top, hands on hips, his red Superman bath towel streaming out behind his shoulders.

"Kevin!" she called. "Mom said you have to come home."

"Can't. I gotta save the world from the Nazis."

Molly kicked the pebbles. "The world can wait. You've got to sweep up in Mom's shop."

"Superman don't clean no beauty shops."

"Mom said to come home now, or she'll have to lock your comics in her closet."

"Shoot!" yelled Kevin, leaping down. "She's always making us work."

He trotted over to where Molly stood waiting. Molly brushed a fleck of sand from his freckled cheek. "You know we've got to help out more with Dad gone, and it's your turn."

"Yeah, I know. But I liked working on Dad's fishing boat better."

"Me too."

Kevin squinted up at her, his blue eyes catching cloud and sun. Did he miss Dad as much as she did? When Dad left a year ago to join the Army Air Corps, Molly was twelve, old enough to understand about the war, but Kevin had been only seven.

She twirled a strand of hair around her finger. "You'd better get on home."

"Yeah, okay." Kevin pivoted and hurried down the beach, his cape billowing out behind him as he ran.

Molly skirted the climbing rocks and hiked another

mile down the shore to the trailhead. She searched the bayberry bushes for her tin bucket, stopped to fill it with salt water, and headed up the path to St. George's Ruin.

Sunlight patched the forest floor as she climbed. Molly breathed in the salty air, moving in rhythm to the waves below. Halfway up the hill, she turned off the trail, plunged into the underbrush, and tore a ribbon off a fir tree. Dad would have hated to see these markers here. The Gainsville Lumber Mill had no right to log timber so close to the ruin. She tore the rest of the markers from the firs, five in all, stuffing them into her pocket.

Emerging from the woods, she hiked to the top and looked across the wide cliff. The old stone walls of St. George's Ruin cast jagged shadows across the ground. Wind whistled through two gaping windows that stared like hollow giant's eyes across the gray Atlantic.

Molly never tired of looking at the ruin. It was a magic place. Her dad had always said so. It had felt strange at first to come up here alone after he shipped out. So much of her dad was up here. Sometimes it seemed as if he'd pop out from behind a tree any minute, grab her, and laugh. "Got ya, little bird."

Stashing her bucket in the juniper bushes, she crawled to the edge of the cliff and looked down. Twenty years ago a whole section of Keenan Cliff had broken away. The back wall of St. George's Church had crashed down to the shore below. A giant stone cross, broken by the fall, lay atop the stones that had once been the back wall of the church. Chin in hand, Molly watched long green flags of seaweed flutter as wave after wave washed over the cross.

Scooting backward, she sat up and looked at Keenan town below. Sturdy wood houses lined the narrow streets from the rocky shore up to the tree-lined hills. At the far end of the cove, lobster boats dotted the harbor. The boats looked as small as toys from her place on the cliff. She held up her thumb and covered the docks. One of the boats was her dad's, but she couldn't tell which one it was from here.

Dad hadn't fished for a long time. He was miles from Maine, stationed in England, piloting his Thunderbolt across enemy lines. He'd been gone a year now. And her chest ached with a slow, deep pain whenever she thought of him.

The day before he'd shipped out, he'd taken her up to the cliff to watch the sunrise. She remembered the way the gulls had looked, flying windward, hanging still as puppets from their strings. She'd tilted her head back to watch the rolling clouds.

Dad scooted closer. "What are you looking at?"

"A chariot."

"I see it," said Dad, looking across the water at the sun-streaked clouds. "And two horses."

"Do you have to go?" asked Molly suddenly.

"Yes."

Molly bit her lip and kept her eyes on the chariot. Who would come up to the ruin to watch the sunrise with her when he was gone? Who would ask her what she saw in the clouds?

"Don't be sad, Molly May," said Dad, reaching into his coat to pull out his pocket watch. He ran his thumb along the letter "F" engraved on the gold cover, then flipped open the hunting case. Molly leaned closer, looking at the tiny Roman numerals, the spot on the face that displayed the phases of the moon. Today the moon was crescent-shaped.

"I want you to have something," said Dad. Tugging the chain free, he dangled it above her hand and coiled it slowly into her palm. She stared down at it, surprised.

"Bet you didn't expect me to give you that, did you, Molly?" He gave her shoulder a squeeze. "Our time together has to stop for a while, but when I come home, I'll put the chain back on my watch, and we'll start right where we left off. Meanwhile, I know you'll keep my chain in a safe place for me."

Molly nodded and closed her fingers around the gold chain. "But what if something happens to you, and you don't . . . I mean—" She swallowed the rest of her words. Far below the cliff, she could hear the waves crashing on the rocks.

"Don't worry, Molly," he said. "Nothing's going to happen to me. I'm a good pilot."

"But all you ever did was crop dusting for Uncle William, and that was a long time ago."

"Long before you were born," said Dad. "But flying is something you never forget." Clouds reflected in his dark brown eyes, as if he were already up there in his plane, cutting through Molly's horses and her chariot.

"They're asking for men with experience," he

said. "It's my chance to help out." He glanced down again and flipped the watch over.

"Open the back," said Molly, scooting closer. Dad pried open the gold hunting case, revealing the secret place at the back of his watch. "You could hide a message in there," said Molly. "Send me the watch with a note if you get in trouble."

Dad smiled at her, the wet sea wind blowing his dark hair across his brow. "It would have to be a pretty short message, little bird."

It had been a year now since that morning. Dad had flown a lot of missions in his P-47 Thunderbolt. He'd even been shot down once after battling five Messerschmitts. He'd bailed out of his burning plane over the English Channel, was rescued by the RAF, and was awarded the Silver Star for valor.

All year long Molly had kept his watch chain tucked away in her desk drawer. If they let him come home for Christmas, she'd pull out the chain and show him how she'd kept her promise.

Molly put her hand to her cheek.

"Christmas."

She said the word to the wind that blew out over the water, to the spruce trees that swayed in that same wind, and to the sunlight that fell in bright patches across St. George's Ruin.

Humming to herself, she grasped her water bucket and went to her digging spot. The church was hollow. Three tumbledown walls, no roof, but there was treasure here.

The stained-glass window on the far-right wall had shattered when the cliff fell, leaving a gaping five-foot-square hole in the stone wall. Twenty years of leaves and mud had covered the fallen glass. A month ago she'd come up here alone after her friend Grace had moved to Virginia. She'd paced beside the ruin, kicking up the dirt, and discovered her first piece of blue glass poking out of the soil at the base of the wall. Since that day, she'd dug up enough to fill a box hidden beneath her bed.

Removing the branches that covered her hole, she pulled the cleaning rag and mashed-potato spoon from her sweater pocket and began to dig.

A squirrel chattered overhead as she scooped the soft dirt with the rusty spoon. Molly fingered the cool earth. Clumps of dirt, a few rocks, twigs. She flung the dirt aside and dug again. This time she uncovered two squarish pieces of glass. She laid them aside, sure that when she washed them they would turn out to be a deep green like many other pieces she'd found.

She dug deeper. No glass, but the digging eased her mind. When she found all the pieces, she'd glue the stained glass onto an old window that was hidden up in her attic. A stained-glass window from St. George's would make a perfect Christmas present for her dad.

Her next scoop yielded an almond-shaped piece of glass. She held it carefully in her hand, wondering what color it would be. Laying it aside, she forced herself to wash the two square pieces first. Both were dark green, as she expected. Grasping the almond-shaped piece, she plunged her hand into the water pail and rubbed the mud off with her rag.

Molly's throat tightened as the dirt slowly washed away from the glass. She was looking at an eye. From under the water the eye was looking back at her.

Beach Fire

The stained-glass eye was long and narrow with a fiery golden slit for a pupil, like the eye of a reptile.

Molly's tongue felt dry and bitter. What would the eye of a reptile be doing in a church window? Maybe it was a picture of the Garden of Eden, with animals, trees, and a serpent. Molly had already fit together three pale bits of glass that resembled a man's face. The man could be Adam. But where were all the other animals? And where was Eve?

She plunged her spoon in again, feeling the muscles in her arm tense as she dug. What was she looking for? More animal eyes, or the face of a woman? The eye on the torn rag by her knee seemed to be watching her. She looked away, ran her hand through another pile of dirt. Nothing.

Molly dug for another half hour until the hole beneath the crumbling wall was broad and deep. Satisfied she'd found all she could, she wrapped the glass in her rag, stuffed it in her pocket, and dumped her water bucket. After carefully filling in the hole, she started for the path that led down to the shore.

A heavy fog was rolling in off the ocean. It fingered blindly through the trees, catching the summer sunlight before it hit the forest floor. Wet mist cooled her cheeks as she reached the base of the trail and ran down the beach toward home.

She would have run right past the boy beside the crackling fire if she hadn't seen him drop a dollar bill into the flames.

Crazy. What was he doing burning money, especially in the middle of the war, when it was so scarce? Before he could spot her, Molly slipped behind a boulder, leaned against the wet rock, and watched him circle the fire.

The boy's back was to her now. He was dark haired like her father. Tall, long legged. She guessed he was about her age, thirteen, maybe fourteen. As he turned aside, Molly saw his face. Peter Birmingham, the rich boy whose dad owned the only department store in Keenan. What was he doing home? Peter was usually away at a boarding school. He rarely came back to Keenan, even in the summer.

She watched him reach into a leather schoolbag.

Extracting a small black book, he ripped the pages out one by one, and threw them on the fire. Then he stood back, crossed his arms, and smiled.

Molly stood very still as Peter reached into the bag again, this time pulling out a striped tie. He turned and held it over the fire. A sickening thrill raced through her as yellow flames licked up the tie toward his hand.

She sucked in a breath, expecting to see Peter's sleeve catch fire, but he dropped the tie just in time.

Stepping back, he took a flying leap over the flames and spun round. His eyes narrowed as he caught sight of her. "What do you want?"

"Nothing."

"Well, go home, then! This is my fire!"

Molly stepped forward and dug the toes of her sneakers into the pebbles. "I can stay if I want to. It's a free beach!"

A sandpiper scuttled past, taking wing before it reached the boulders. Peter shoved his hands into his pockets. "Nothing's free. Don't you know that?"

Molly's jaw tightened. What did he know? The sea, the birds, the trees, everything that mattered was free. She gazed at the school clothes that hung loosely on his tall frame as he poked the fire.

Flames leaped up, pulsing with heat. Molly bent to toss a driftwood stick into the flames. The fire popped, sending a handful of sparks into the air.

Peter looked at her, his eyebrows arching as if he were studying a painting. "So," he said. "What's your name?"

"Molly."

"Sorry. I mean, I've seen you around town, but I'm away at boarding school most of the year, so . . ." He paused. "You live across the street from my dad's store, don't you?"

"Yeah."

"Your mom has a beauty parlor on the first floor of your house, right? My mom goes there to get her hair done."

"I know. I've seen her." Molly looked into the fire, not sure what to say next. She waited awhile, the sea pounding the shore behind her, then began to scan the dancing light for dragons. There were always dragons in the fire if you looked closely enough. Her dad had taught her that. At last she settled on a driftwood branch arched like a dragon's back with red-hot scales. She squinted into the flames but couldn't see the dragon's face.

A crow landed on Peter's schoolbag and pecked at something shiny beneath a wool scarf. Another crow landed, then another.

"Scat!" shouted Peter, running at them.

Caw! Caw! The crows flew up and dove again. Molly covered her head as Peter waved a stick to fight them off. Caw! Caw! They flapped noisily into the fog.

Molly laughed. "You make a pretty good scarecrow."

Peter shrugged. "Thanks."

"Crows can't resist shiny things." Molly knelt down and picked up the small treasure the birds had uncovered. It was a Christmas ornament. A tin angel.

She held it near the fire. Flames flashed gold on its wings. "This won't burn," she said quietly.

Peter frowned, his dark bangs blowing across his high forehead. "Take it if you like," he said.

"Really?"

"Sure, I don't care."

She put the angel in her pocket by the stained-glass bundle. "Thanks," she said, standing up to brush off the tiny pebbles that were sticking to her pants. "Well, I've got to get going."

"Your family expecting you for dinner?"

"My mom, grandma, and kid brother. My dad's away. You know, fighting in the war."

"Army?"

"No. He's a fighter pilot stationed over in England. Been gone a year. But he's coming home for Christmas." Molly bit her lip. Why did she tell him that? She hadn't meant to tell anyone her secret wish. She turned to leave.

"Hey, wait," said Peter, pointing to the ribbons that now trailed from her pocket. "What've you got there?"

"Nothing."

He stepped closer, his leather shoes nearly touching her sneakers. "I know what those are," he said.

The stolen ribbons fluttered in the breeze.

"So?"

"So where'd you get them?"

Molly eyed the pile spilling out of his school-bag. "I'll tell you where I got the ribbons, if you tell me why you're burning those things."

Peter stepped back, jammed his hands into his pockets, and stared out to sea.

The sun was setting behind the mountains. It tinted the fog pink above the water. Molly wrapped a strand of red hair around her finger. Peter had secrets. He was full of secrets.

"What are you gonna do with those ribbons?" he asked.

"I don't know." She thought of the beautiful fir and spruce forest near the ruin the Gainsville Lumber Mill had selected to cut.

"These aren't ribbons," she announced. "They're the flags of my enemy!"

"Then burn them," said Peter, his wide mouth breaking into a smile. "Use my fire."

Molly tore the ribbons from her pocket. They twisted and flailed in the sea breeze like frantic fish.

Peter kicked a piece of driftwood deeper into the flames. Sparks leaped into the air. "What are you waiting for?" he asked.

She threw a ribbon on the fire. The damp end sizzled. The dry end flew into flame.

"For the beautiful firs!" she shouted.

"For the beautiful firs!" echoed Peter.

Molly held another tree marker in the air and let the tip catch fire. "For old St. George's!" she called.

"For St. George and the dragon!" shouted Peter.

The marker crackled like a dry leaf as the fire licked up the edges.

"Peter!" a man's voice called through the fog.

"Drop it!" cried Peter, falling to his knees to thrust the pile of loot back in his schoolbag.

Flames wove up the ribbon, moving closer to her

hand. "I said drop it! Someone's coming!"

Peter was still kicking sand and pebbles into the fire when a tall man came up the beach, pushed a clump of seaweed aside with a stick, and peered at him through thick glasses. "I've been sent to call you in for dinner, though I can assure you fetching boys for their meals is not part of my job description."

"Molly," said Peter, "this is my father's personal secretary, Mr. Avery."

Mr. Avery gave her a quick nod. "Afternoon, young lady."

"Hello."

"Dinner's waiting, and it's getting cold as we speak."

Peter wiped his hands on his jeans. "Where are Mom and Dad?"

"They went out."

"We were going to have dinner together tonight. Where'd they go this time?"

"I don't know. Your father was upset before he left. He couldn't find his appointment book."

Mr. Avery squinted at a small piece of black leather poking out of the smoldering pile. Peter squared his jaw and stepped in front of it.

"Well," said Mr. Avery. "Come on, then."

Peter grabbed his schoolbag, took a last look at Molly, and followed Mr. Avery up the beach.

At home, Molly curled up in her dad's old leather chair, the smell of boiled cabbage wafting from the kitchen. She unfolded Sergeant Murphy's letter, but didn't bother to read it. She'd read the letter more than a hundred times and knew every word by heart. Still, she liked to look at Sergeant Murphy's awkward script telling about her dad's heroic battle over France. How he'd protected the damaged B-17 from five enemy aircraft and lost his Thunderbolt over the English Channel.

Dad had sent them V-Mail about the incident. But he'd downplayed the whole thing. Sergeant Murphy's letter told the whole story and praised her dad as a hero. She put the letter down, ran her hand along the smooth black leather, found the tear on the edge of the armrest, and tugged on the oily thread.

From the picture on the mantel, Dad looked down at her. He was in full uniform, standing by his Thunderbolt, *Lucky Seven*. The photo had been taken a few days before *Lucky Seven* was shot down.

Molly looked into her dad's face, his easy smile, his dark eyes that seemed to twinkle at her as if he were just about to tell a joke. She slipped her hand into her pocket and smiled back at the photo. Dad would come home for Christmas; she was sure of that now. He'd put the star on top of the tree, and when all the rest of the decorations were on, she'd pull out the angel Peter had given her and hang it just below the star.

She wrapped her fingers around the angel. It was a sign, a small promise with tin wings.

"Dinner!" called Grandma.

Molly put the letter back on the mantel beside Dad's photo and took her place beside Kevin at the dining-room table.

Mom came in with a steaming bowl of cabbage. "Put the comic book away, Kevin."

"But, Mom, Superman's gonna use his X-ray vision to—"

"Put it away, now."

"Yes, ma'am." Kevin shoved his comic under his chair, leaned back, and crossed his arms. Across the table, Grandma spread a thin layer of butter on each slice of bread.

Mashed potatoes, cabbage, Spam. Molly was sick of eating the cabbage from Grandma's Victory garden, sick of mashed potatoes, and sicker still of Spam. When the war was over, they'd eat real meat, not meat from a can. They'd buy their vegetables from Henson's Market, and she'd spread huge hunks of butter on her bread.

"Eat your vegetables, honey," said Mom.

Kevin gave Molly a mashed-potato grin as she speared a forkful of boiled cabbage. It smelled faintly like the school rest room. She chewed the bite quickly and washed it down with a gulp of milk.

Grandma spent hours every day digging, weeding, and watering the Victory garden out back. She was devoted to her garden the way her daughter was devoted to her beauty salon. Both women were proud of how they were keeping the family afloat while Dad was away. On the far side of the table, Grandma beamed over her cabbage. Molly stared at the watery green leaves on her plate, trying to work up the right expression. She should smile, tell her the cabbage was wonderful.

"Grandma."

"Yes, dear?"

"The cabbage is . . . "

Grandma looked at her expectantly.

"Could you pass the salt?" said Molly.

There was a loud knock on the front door.

"I'll get it," cried Kevin.

Mom grabbed his arm. "Stay put. I'll go." She went to the window, peeled back the edge of the blackout curtain, and peered outside.

"Who is it?" called Kevin.

Mom turned the dead bolt with a loud *click*, and opened the door.

A tall man in a black coat stood on the front porch looking down at her. "Mrs. George Fowler?"

"Yes?"

"Telegram."

Molly bunched her napkin into a tight ball.

"Is it from Dad?" asked Kevin, his fingers wiggling excitedly. "Is he comin' home from the war?"

Grandma grabbed his hand. "Keep still, Kevin."

"Sign here." Mom signed the form on the clipboard. The stranger gave her a thin piece of paper, touched the brim of his hat, and clumped down the porch steps.

Mom leaned against the closed door reading the yellow paper again and again, her mouth moving inaudibly as if she were speaking underwater.

"What is it, Gail?" Grandma asked.

"Plane shot down over Holland," she mumbled, coming back to the table to slide into her chair. "'Eye-

witnesses observed crash. No parachute seen . . . '"
She breathed quickly, cheeks pale.

"Is Dad a hero?" asked Kevin.

"'We regret to inform you, your husband, Lieutenant George Fowler . . .'"

Molly leaned into the edge of the table, her heart fluttering wildly against her ribs like some desperate caged bird. Don't say it, Mom. Don't say the word.

three

Ashes

Mom laid the telegram on the table. "George is dead," she cried.

"Da-Dad?" sputtered Kevin, his words spilling out hard and uneven as pebbles. He stumbled into his mother's arms and buried his head in her dress.

"Oh, my poor, dear girl," said Grandma as she bent over Molly's mother.

Molly grabbed the telegram. It wasn't true. It couldn't be true. But the words were there, informing them that Dad's plane was shot down. She bit her lip as she read the last four lines: EYEWITNESSES OBSERVED CRASH STOP NO PARACHUTE SEEN STOP LIEUTENANT GEORGE FOWLER PRESUMED DEAD STOP WE ARE

SORRY FOR YOUR LOSS STOP. Molly's insides dried to dust. Her skin felt thin, stretched out like a balloon.

"Molly?" Grandma said, reaching out her hand. "Are you all right?"

Molly dropped the telegram. She stood up, surprised that her legs still worked, and slowly made her way to the stairs. She had to leave. Had to get away from that telegram. That stupid, lying telegram!

Floating up the steps, she locked her bedroom door and leaned against it, staring at the tiny gray particles that danced in the air. She'd never been able to see those particles before. Millions of them. Dancing. She could feel them, too, prickling the skin on her face, arms, and legs.

Downstairs, Mom was sobbing. Kevin's cries came out in little yelps, like a dog with a crushed tail.

Molly wasn't going to cry.

"Dad's not dead," she whispered. The words came from outside of her, as if someone else in the room had spoken them.

Her face was numb. She touched her fingers to her lips and felt the warm breath spill out over them.

"Dad's not dead," she said a little louder. The voice came from inside her this time.

Molly lit a candle, took a small box from her desk drawer, and pulled out the watch chain.

Her dad couldn't be dead, because she would have known. The moment he died, she would have felt it. Strong, like a bullet ripping through her belly, or dark, like a blackout.

She let the watch chain coil into her open palm like a serpent. Outside, the apple tree was shadowed in the twilight. If her legs felt stronger, she'd climb out her window right now, escape down the tree, then run, across the yard, down the steps all the way to the sea. Instead she sat perfectly still, watching the wax slowly drip down the candle and spread onto her desk. The clear pool grew like a small rain puddle, hardening into a white disk. She peeled the wax from the wood and held it to her cheek. It was hard and soft at the same time, like the rubber face on her old doll, Maggie.

The door closed downstairs. Voices. More crying. More voices. By the time she heard a gentle tapping on her door, the candle had burned down to a stub. She blew out the flame. Dark. They'd think she was asleep.

"Molly?" called Grandma. "Dr. Richards has come over. He has given your mother something to calm her nerves. He wants to see you."

Molly didn't answer.

"Molly," Dr. Richards's voice broke in. "I have something here to help you sleep. Please let me in."

"I don't need anything. I'm all right."

"Let us in, dear," said Grandma. "It's for the best."

Molly placed the chain back in the tissue, shoved the box deep into the drawer, and unlocked her door. She still had the wax disk in her hand when Dr. Richards stepped in. He switched on the light, his black-rimmed glasses glinting in the sudden glare. "What's all this about sitting alone in the dark?"

"I like the dark," answered Molly truthfully. "Right, Grandma?"

Grandma stood strangely silent in the broad shadow of the doctor.

"We . . . we like candles at our house. Tell him, Grandma." Grandma stared at Molly, her arms crossed against her aproned chest.

Dr. Richards leaned over and touched Molly's hand. His breath smelled of cooked onions. "Skin's very cold," he remarked. "The news of her father's death may have put her in shock."

Molly pulled away. "I'm not in shock, and I'm not cold. Not cold at all. Tell him! Tell him to leave me alone, Grandma!"

"Bring up some extra blankets, Mrs. Turner."

Grandma left the room.

"You shouldn't make Grandma go up and down the stairs," said Molly. "Her legs give her a lot of pain, especially at night."

"It's all right, Molly. Your grandmother wants to help you." Dr. Richards took a syringe out of his black bag and filled it with fluid from a little bottle. "We just want to make you feel better."

"I'm fine." Molly backed toward the window.

Dr. Richards turned his back, held the syringe in the air, and flicked the glass with his fingertips.

Molly turned the latch, pushed the window open, and slipped one leg over the sill. She'd climb down the tree and run!

Grandma staggered in with a pile of blankets. "Doctor! Stop her!" she screamed.

Dr. Richards grabbed Molly's arm and yanked her back into the room.

"I'm sorry, Doctor," said Grandma over Molly's screams. "She's usually a very cooperative girl. It's the news. The shock of it."

Molly struggled to free herself as he inserted the needle into her upper arm. Dr. Richards eased her onto her bed, where she kicked and kicked until her legs slowed and the air began to grow thick and green all around her. She was swimming away from them, away from Dr. Richards, Grandma. The room slowly swelled with water.

Molly fought her way out of a heavy sleep. Something was wrong, terribly wrong. Her eyes opened to the dark, and she remembered. A telegram had come. It said her dad was dead. She got out of bed, her body still slow and heavy from the shot Dr. Richards had given her. She stepped into the hall. The house was quiet.

Downstairs, Molly rummaged through the dark closet till her fingers found a rough wool collar. Her father's old coat. She slipped it on and lifted the sleeve to her nose. Sharp smells of seaweed and pipe tobacco filled her nostrils. She tiptoed into the kitchen, picked up the telegram that lay on the table beside the bread basket, and padded across the tile floor to the window.

Down the street a dog howled. Another joined in, then another. The sound echoed through Keenan town, out to the cliffs, down to the sea.

Molly folded the telegram into a tiny paper air-plane and placed it in the sink.

The match caught fire with one strike against the stone cutting board. Molly touched the flame to the little yellow plane. The edges burned, slowly turning the paper to a fine gray ash. She watched with deep satisfaction as bits of ash drifted into the air like tiny, tattered moths.

Explosion in the Classroom

Smells of floor wax and wood-oil soap filled Molly's nose as she entered the eighth-grade classroom on the first day of school. Clutching her binder, she walked halfway up the aisle and hesitated. Last year, she and Grace had sat near the front of the class, but this year, Grace was gone, to Virginia. And this year Molly was "the war hero's kid." Eyes to the floor, she headed for the back row. She'd be safer back there. This way, if kids wanted to stare at her, whisper behind their hands in class, they'd have to turn around to do it.

Placing her binder on a back corner desk, she slid into her chair and stared out the window. It had been nearly three weeks since the telegram, and Sunday was her dad's memorial service. Molly didn't want to go. To go would be to admit her dad was dead, and she couldn't admit that. She could never admit that. The telegram had said "presumed dead."

"Presumed." Last week she'd looked the word up in the dictionary. The definition read, "to *suppose* to be true." It hadn't said, "truth, fact." She'd brought the dictionary downstairs to show Grandma. Grandma had rubbed her shoulder, saying, "I know the news about your dad is hard for you to accept, honey. Why don't you help me knead this bread dough. Might help you to feel a little better."

She'd left Grandma leaning over the table, flour up to her elbows. She hadn't wanted to feel better. She'd wanted someone else to understand. Just because no one had seen the parachute didn't mean Dad was dead. Maybe there were clouds in the way. Maybe he'd bailed out at the last moment when no one was looking. They shouldn't give up hope. Not yet.

The bell rang. Kids circled around the desks like bees in a clover patch. Which seat? This one? No, this one. Jane Larkin entered the classroom. Molly tensed, hoping Jane wouldn't come her way. But Jane was a back-row girl. She turned and headed right for the seat across from Molly. Jane put her old stained binder on her desk and sat down, giving Molly a quick glance before pulling out her pencil.

Spotting an empty desk one row up, Molly grabbed her binder to make her move, but Mary Pringle slipped into the seat. Too late.

Classmates leaned over their desks, talking to their friends. Molly made moon-shaped nail marks in her big pink eraser and tried not to look at Jane. There was always a lot to gossip about in Keenan, but Jane's story was the most exotic, and she'd heard the whole story in her mom's salon. What other child in Keenan was born out of wedlock? What other child had a mysterious father from the Orient? Jane's mother met him working one summer in an Alaskan cannery. The story was rich with mystery, and gossips like Dee Brown loved it.

Jane's mom had left her in Keenan and came home to visit her daughter only once a year. Her grandparents, Daniel and May Larkin, had done their best to raise Jane, but things had taken a turn for the worse when Daniel died at sea. Molly turned her eraser over. May Larkin had never been the same after her husband's death. The harder things got for Jane, the more the town gossips had to talk about, and Molly had heard it all as Mom cut and permed her customers' hair.

The late bell rang. Mrs. LaCasse entered the classroom and headed for the bookshelf. "Good morning, class," she said, pulling out a stack of math books.

"Good morning, Mrs. LaCasse."

She passed the books around. "We'll be spending the first few days of class assessing your skill levels in each subject," she said as she went up and down the aisles. "Let's see what you've forgotten over the summer."

"I've forgotten everything," said Sam.

"No doubt you have, Sam Henson."

Robbie Devlin snorted. Sam flashed him a sharp look.

Molly opened her math book and worked the review problems. She paused to tug the sleeve of her sweater down to the tips of her fingers. It made her pencil look as if it were sprouting out of a tiny hollow log. They'd keep all the classrooms cool this year like they had the last: Part of the war effort not to use too much fuel. She wished she'd picked the corner desk by the heater, but Sam had claimed it. He was leaning peacefully toward the clanking radiator. The tips of his ears were red. He actually looked hot.

Sam caught her looking at him and narrowed his eyes. She turned away, heart beating. It wasn't a good idea to stir things up with Sam. He'd been a bully ever since fourth grade, when his parents had split up. She didn't want to be one of his targets again this year.

Pencils scratched. Mrs. LaCasse's high heels clicked against the floor as she crossed the room to answer questions. Molly was on her tenth problem when she noticed Sam signaling Joe. Out of the corner of her eye she saw Sam reach into his pocket. Just then, Joe's hand shot up. "Mrs. LaCasse? I don't understand what they want me to do with this problem."

Mrs. LaCasse leaned over Joe's paper. "Well, you . . . "

With the teacher's back turned, Sam deftly unwrapped a foil packet and placed some small objects on top of the radiator. *POP! BANG! POW! POP! BANG!*

"Japanese!" screamed Robbie.

The whole class leaped out of their chairs and dove under their desks. Joe ran to the window, shouting, "Where? Where?"

Mary Pringle screamed. Sally Pratt threw up on the floor.

"Stop!" cried Mrs. LaCasse. Facing the radiator, she noted the telltale stream of smoke rising delicately to the ceiling. The radiator, as if in final betrayal, let off one last *BANG!*

Swooping down, Mrs. LaCasse caught Sam's ear and yanked him out from under his desk. Sam crouched in pain as she dragged him to the cloakroom.

"Joe," she called. "Help Sally to the office! And Jane, get the bucket and clean up that vomit!"

Everyone took their seats, whispering to one another as Mrs. LaCasse lectured Sam in the cloakroom. Molly sat, chin in hand, watching Jane out of the corner of her eye, her jet-black hair veiling her face as she wiped the vomit off the floor. Ever since the bombing of Pearl Harbor, rumors about Jane's background had gotten worse. People were now saying Jane's father was Japanese. No one had any proof, but that didn't seem to matter. Everyone had started to think of her as the enemy. Adults kept their distance. Some kids, like Sam, pushed her around, calling her Jane-the-Jap. May Larkin, lost in her own world, had been unable to fend off the ugly stories.

Leaving Sam to think over his sins in the cloak-room, Mrs. LaCasse returned to her desk. "Open your math books and continue working," she ordered.

Molly flipped her book open, covering her nose as Jane passed with the soggy mop reeking of vomit. Through the door of the cloakroom, Sam glared at Molly as she watched Jane slip into the hall.

"Jap lover," he mouthed.

After school, Molly leaned against the willow tree at the edge of the playground and waited for Kevin. The sea wind blew a gray trail of smoke above the rooftops. The smoke drifted over the hill and across the grassy field. The grass was brown and bent now. But in summer the grass had stood tall, blowing in golden waves that rattled as you walked through them.

A flock of starlings twittered and sang in the giant maple at the far end of the field. Leaves fluttered in the breeze, their tips as red as match heads. The family had a picnic under that tree the day before Dad left for the Army Air Corps. Had they eaten deviled egg sandwiches or tuna? Molly couldn't remember. Right after lunch, Dad had pulled out his camera. "Stop wiping your nose, Kevin," he said. "And Molly, stand closer to your mom. That's it." He snapped the photo of the three of them beneath the maple tree.

"Okay, Molly!" Dad called, putting his camera away. "You're it!"

Molly covered her eyes and counted, " . . . ninety-eight, ninety-nine, one-hundred. Ready or not. Here I come!" Turning around, she ran up the hill. First she spotted Mom's blue scarf, fluttering in the tall grass. "One-two-three on Mom!" she called. Then Kevin sneezed and gave himself away.

"No fair!" he shouted. "Just 'cause I'm allergic! I should get to hide again!"

Dad was the hardest one to find. Molly had looked everywhere, her heart pounding to the beat of her running feet. She searched and searched, trying to spot Dad's jet-black hair in the cream-colored grass.

"Tell him to come out," said Mom with a laugh.

"No," insisted Molly. "I'll find him."

Dad always won the game. She wouldn't let him win this time. She'd find him. Swish. Swish. Molly hacked at the grass with the side of her hand as she ran, her breath coming in hot, dry gulps.

"Home free!" shouted Dad as he dashed back to the maple tree. "I won!"

Molly tugged on a drooping willow branch and squinted up at the sky. The sun was a white disk hiding behind thick clouds.

Hide-and-seek.

Was Dad in hiding? Where? Was he in enemy-occupied Holland? Moving only by night? Trying to make it to safety?

Or had he been picked up by the Germans? Was he in a prison camp, keeping the watch hidden until he could send a message to her?

A shiver traced her spine from tailbone to neck.

Come out, come out, wherever you are . . .

On the hill above the school, Jane's grandmother appeared, her faded shawl draped thin as a spider's web over her gray hair. Mrs. Larkin used to teach foreign languages to seventh and eighth graders at Keenan School, but she stopped working after her husband died at sea. Kids said she went crazy after that, started staring out the window all the time and talking to herself in class. When she was caught lighting beacon fires on Keenan Cliff, Principal Wierman fired her.

Jane closed the back gate and climbed the path to meet her grandmother. Together they headed up the hill behind the school, Jane's hair fluttering in the breeze like blackbird wings.

"Wake up," shouted Kevin, tossing a rock at Molly's feet.

"I'll show you who's awake!" Molly chased Kevin all the way to Quincy Avenue. Darting past town hall, they raced down the hill to Keenan Harbor, then slowed to a walk on Main Street.

"Kevin?" said Molly as they walked past Dee Brown's bright yellow house.

"Yeah?"

"You think Mrs. Larkin is strange?"

"Sure she is! All the kids think so."

"Why?"

Kevin stopped by Fitzhenry's Marine Supplies and leaned against a stack of lobster traps. "Why what?"

"Why do they think she's strange?"

"Jeeze! What's the matter with you, Molly? She talks to herself. She lights those fires on top of Keenan Cliff in the middle of the night."

Molly skirted the shop and walked out along the creaking dock. Kevin followed. She could see Mr. Fitzhenry peering at them from inside the marine supply shop, but she turned toward the harbor, spotting Dad's boat, the *Molly May*, in the rippling water. "Mrs. Larkin doesn't light those beacon fires on the cliff anymore, Kev. Not since the war started. Besides," she said, "what's so bad about that? Women have lit beacon fires for centuries to help guide lost sailors home."

Kevin waved his hands above his head like an animated scarecrow. "That's nuts. Everybody in Keenan knows Mr. Larkin isn't lost. He died at sea five years ago!"

Molly toed a coiled rope on the dock. "Listen, Kev, people aren't always right about . . . about things."

She took a sharp breath, if she wasn't careful, she'd tell Kevin her thoughts about Dad. "Maybe he is alive!" she blurted, her eyes flitting across Kevin's freckled face.

Kevin's cheeks turned suddenly pale.

"Daniel Larkin, I mean. He could be alive somewhere. Mrs. Larkin could just be trying to bring him home. Maybe she's right, and everybody else in Keenan is wrong."

Kevin's jaw dropped. He blinked at Molly as if taking sudden snapshots of her face. "Go to the graveyard, stupid. Mr. Larkin's gravestone's there."

Molly knew she should drop the subject. Kevin

34

got upset so easily. Ever since the telegram came, he'd fight about anything.

"That doesn't prove a thing, Kev. Mr. Larkin's boat was never found. You know there's no body in that grave. It's nothing but dirt and worms."

"Shut up, Molly!" Kevin grabbed her sweater. "Just shut up about it. You're talking crazy!" He twisted the wool collar around his small fist.

"Let go of me!"

"Not till you take it back about Mr. Larkin!"

"I won't take it back! There's no body in that grave!"

"Shut your mouth!"

Molly pushed Kevin away. He reeled back, taking great gulps of air. Then he turned and ran up the dock, whacking the lobster traps as he raced by. Two traps tumbled onto the ground.

"Hey!" shouted Mr. Fitzhenry, poking his head out the door.

"Sorry," said Molly, coming ashore to restack the traps.

Traps secure, she started up Main Street. A wisp of fog blew in off the water. In the harbor, a buoy bell made a hollow, clanking sound. Molly ran a stick along a sagging fence as she headed for home. People called Mrs. Larkin strange just because she thought her husband was still alive. But what if she was right? What if Mr. Larkin had just gotten tired of Keenan, taken his fishing boat to another port, and run away to start a new life? It might have happened that way. It could be true.

She tossed her stick over the fence into the cord-grass. If she told people she thought her dad was still alive, they'd tell stories about her, too. They'd say she was crazy like Mrs. Larkin.

Molly felt a clutching in her chest. She breathed against it, trying to loosen the muscles above her breastbone. She wanted so much to talk to someone about her dad, but she couldn't tell Kevin or Mom or Grandma, and there was no one at school.

Crossing the street to avoid passing Henson's Market, she paused by the swirling barbershop pole and pulled the tin angel from her pocket. Peter. She might be able to tell him. They'd shared a fire together, burned secret things on the beach. But then he might have already gone back to boarding school.

A delivery truck rumbled past, turning into the parking lot by Henson's Market. Molly jammed the angel back in her pocket and headed down the block. Soon there'd be another empty grave in Keenan. This Sunday was her dad's memorial service. Well, she wouldn't go. She wasn't going to stand around and watch the town put a tombstone at the head of another empty grave.

five

The Service

Grandma dropped a glob of oatmeal into Molly's bowl and placed the pot back on the stove. Kevin sprinkled two spoons of brown sugar into his hot cereal.

"Whoa, Kevin," said Grandma. "We don't have enough ration coupons to waste our sugar like that."

Kevin bit his lip, the sugar in his bowl melting into muddy brown splashes.

Grandma patted his shoulder. "I'm sorry, honey. I know you're upset about the service today. Just be more careful with the food, okay?"

Mom came into the kitchen and poured herself a cup of coffee. Her red hair was in curlers, and her thin cheeks looked drawn without the usual rouge.

Molly took a bite of oatmeal. It tasted like wet sawdust. She wanted to leave. Go upstairs, outside, anywhere. It was hard to stay in the kitchen with her grandma's worried face. Mom's puffy eyes. Kevin's drooping lip.

The clock on the stove ticked like a time bomb. She watched her brother finish his bowl. He wiped his mouth with the back of his hand and headed upstairs to get changed.

"I laid your clothes out on your bed," Grandma called up after him. Kevin's door slammed.

"You'd better get changed, too, honey," said Mom, "so Grandma has time to braid your hair."

Molly traced the checkerboard tablecloth—red, white, red. "I'm not putting on that dress," she said absently.

"I know it's too big for you, dear, but your great-aunt Sara took the trouble to send it to us all the way from . . . Molly, are you listening to me?"

Molly hopped her finger to another red square and looked up.

"Anyway," continued Mom, "you have to wear black to a funeral."

"It's not a funeral. There's no body."

Mom's cheeks reddened as if she'd just been slapped. "That doesn't make any difference, memorial service, or whatever you call it. Anyway, you still have to wear black."

Molly pushed her chair away from the table and stood up. "I don't need to wear the dress, because I'm not going."

"Not going? What do you mean?"

"I'm not going to the memorial service." She twisted the belt of her robe around her hand, tight, tighter. "Everyone in this town is crazy. Just because we got a stupid little piece of yellow paper, everyone is acting like Daddy's dead!"

Mom stood up shakily.

"The telegram said he was shot down," said Molly. "But he was shot down before, and he was okay. Maybe he bailed out in time."

There! The truth was out! It was just a mistake. Dad was alive.

Mom leaned over the table, her face salt white. "No one saw a parachute."

"Cloudy," said Molly. "It could have been too cloudy to see the chute from the sky." She was talking too fast now, saying all the things she'd thought about the past three weeks but hadn't had the courage to say. "Dad could have landed in enemy territory and been picked up by the Nazis. He could be a POW and—"

"POWs are reported, Molly. The Army Air Corps would have heard by now. They would have—"

"Not always, I mean . . . or he could be hiding out, trying to get out of Holland."

Mom brought her hand to her lips. "I know you don't want to believe it, Molly," she gulped. "None of us want to believe it. I wish to God . . ." She slumped down in her chair and put her face in her hands.

Seeing her mom crumpled, shaking, made

Molly's knees soft as putty. She could feel the blood pulsing in her hand where the belt was twisted.

Grandma placed a protective hand on her daughter's shoulder and looked up at Molly. "You're a part of this family, young lady. Go upstairs now and put on your dress."

"But, Grandma—"

"Go!"

Molly ran upstairs, slammed her door, and leaned against it. She was shaking now, ashamed, alone. Dad wouldn't have liked her treating Mom that way. He would have done what Grandma did, sent her to her room, made her comply. But how could she go? How could she sit through the memorial service? Stand by that gravestone?

She closed her eyes and saw the image of her mom, face in hands, and knew she had to go. Not because Grandma ordered her to, but because she couldn't hurt her mom again.

It doesn't mean anything, she told herself. Just because I'm going. It doesn't mean I think he's dead.

Crossing the room, she pulled the cardboard box out from under her bed and looked at her stained-glass collection. Still unsure of what the old window had looked like before the landslide, she'd left the pieces in the box, waiting for the courage to begin gluing them together.

Molly closed her eyes and fingered through the pile of glass.

If I pick red, Daddy's dead.

Her hand suddenly went cold. She was thirteen

years old. Why did her mind still play tricks on her like she was a kid? Touching a small, triangular piece, she pulled it from the pile.

Don't be red. Don't be red.

Molly opened her eyes. It was blue. Her shoulders sank in a sigh.

"Molly," Grandma called up the stairs. "Are you dressed yet?"

"I'll be ready in a minute, Grandma." Molly shoved the box back under her bed and pulled the black dress from its hanger. The fabric was stiff and smelled of mothballs. She removed her robe and nightgown and slipped it on, feeling goose bumps pop up where the crepe touched her flesh.

The organ played softly in St. Luke's Church. All the pews were full. Molly had recognized nearly everyone when she'd walked in. All the kids from school sitting by their parents. All the teachers, fishermen, shopkeepers—everyone from Keenan seemed to be there. Molly knew them all, but there were a few elderly men and women sitting in the back near Jane and her grandmother whom Molly had never seen before. She thought they might be farmers, people who knew her dad when he was a boy growing up outside of Gainsville.

Molly fiddled with her white gloves and took a deep breath: candle wax, perfume, sweat, all familiar church smells. She'd make it through if she pretended it was just another Sunday service. She didn't have to listen to anything Reverend Olson said. She could lose herself in the pattern of the stained-glass window behind the altar. Jesus in the clouds, the angels at his feet singing. But what about after? What about the part where she had to stand beside the gravestone?

The Birminghams came in, walked right up to the front pew across from Molly's family, and sat down. Molly turned and met Peter's dark eyes. His brows lifted. She blushed and faced forward. She was here for her mom. Her mom needed her to sit through this. It didn't mean anything. She wanted Peter to know that.

A ray of purple light fell through the window. Molly followed the shaft as it touched the tip of the cross, cascaded down the choir loft, and came to rest on a tall bouquet of carnations. She took off her glove and felt in her pocket for the piece of blue glass she'd brought. Not red, she reminded herself as Reverend Olson stepped up to the lectern, his back cutting into the ray of purple light. The reverend cleared his throat and leaned over the lectern, staring at the congregation. People coughed, shuffled in their seats. Adjusting his glasses, he said, "Please join with me and sing 'Onward Christian Soldiers,' page two hundred thirty-four in your hymnal."

"Daddy's not a soldier," said Kevin. "He's a fighter-pilot."

"Shhh," warned Mom.

They stood to sing. Molly dutifully marched the words through all three verses till the last note died away, then sat down again, relieved.

Reverend Olson sighed and ran his eye along every row of parishioners. Hymnals were closed and slipped into the backs of the pews again. Everyone hushed.

"We're here today to honor a brave man," he began. "George Fowler was a family man, a fisherman, an ordinary man in many ways, at least that's what we may have thought. But George was no ordinary man. He was a hero. It took a war to show us that." He paused and pulled a letter from his Bible. "I have here a letter from Waist-gunner Sergeant Frank Murphy. Mrs. Fowler wanted me to read it to you today."

He unfolded Sergeant Murphy's letter. Molly clenched her blue glass and looked over at her mom. She hadn't told her Reverend Olson would be reading the letter.

The reverend cleared his throat. "This letter was written seven months before George Fowler's death. It tells the story of the heroism that won George Fowler the Silver Star last February. The letter begins, 'Dear Mrs. Fowler: I'm writing to you and your family from my hospital room. I want you to know I'm alive today because of Lieutenant George Fowler.'"

Molly closed her eyes. She'd read the letter so many times, but she'd never heard it read by a man.

"'Several weeks ago,'" continued Reverend Olson, "'on February 24, 1944, our B-17 was separated from the formation and attacked over France by a swarm of enemy fighters. A blast hit our center section, tearing through the landing gear and wounding Sergeant Mathews and myself. I got a piece of metal in my side and was losing blood fast. With only the Tail-gunner left to defend us, it was just a matter of time before we were hit again. This time the blast damaged our left wing. We lost altitude. With Messerschmitts gunning us from all directions, we thought we were goners, until Lieutenant Fowler saw the mess we were in. He flew down in his Thunderbolt and fought them off one by one as we raced toward home.'"

Molly glanced over at Peter. His eyes were wide, a look of awe on his face.

"'It was one against five,'" continued Reverend Olson, "'but Lieutenant Fowler didn't let up until we were safe. His plane was hit over France. He bailed out over the English Channel a few minutes before our plane hit the runway.'

"'Minutes later, my buddy and I were rushed to the hospital. Both of us made it.'"

Molly tried to swallow, her tongue was too dry, her ears were ringing.

"'After my surgery, I learned the RAF had rescued Lieutenant Fowler from the channel. I have to say I was glad to hear it. I wanted a chance to personally thank the man who saved my life.

"'I'm proud to say I was on the mission that won Lieutenant George Fowler the Silver Star.'"

Reverend Olson looked up, slowly removing his glasses. "My daddy did that," said Kevin. Molly reached over, took his hand, and held it as Reverend Olson talked on about the hardships of war, the sacrifices. She didn't let go until he asked them all to pray.

Mom, Kevin, and Grandma were on their knees. Molly knelt and bowed her head. She'd pray, but not for someone who was dead. She'd ask God for a sign. For some kind of sign.

Rain drumrolled off the umbrellas on the hill above St. Luke's as the people huddled around the grave. Molly watched her mom's high heels sink into the soft earth as she stepped forward and placed a small bouquet of roses on the ground before the gravestone that read:

GEORGE FOWLER DECEMBER 2, 1911–AUGUST 18, 1944
DIED BRAVELY IN THE SERVICE OF HIS COUNTRY.
DEATH TOOK HIM FROM US, BUT HE LIVES ON IN OUR HEARTS.

The words were carved in stone, but Molly knew they were wrong. She squinted, trying to blur the letters as raindrops cascaded down the headstone to the soil at the base.

At last the service had come to an end. One by one, people began to leave. Molly stood beside Grandma, left hand in her sweater pocket touching the smooth surface of blue stained glass, right hand extended to shake people's damp hands.

"So sorry," they said.

"He was such a good man."

She kept her eyes on the empty grave, watching the roses bob up and down in the rain.

Mrs. Larkin stepped up to Molly. Took her hand and gave it a squeeze. She didn't say she was sorry or that her father was a good man. Instead, she looked deep into Molly's eyes, nodding her head up and down as if they shared a secret. Molly dodged her light blue eyes and concentrated on her soggy hat. The lime-green netting was torn near the brim. Someone had tried to fix the tear by stitching on a cloth rosebud.

"Come on, Grandma," said Jane, nudging her along the line. Molly avoided Jane's eyes and looked down at her own crepe dress. The cloth had darkened in the rain, if black could get any darker. Her bare legs poking out beneath the stiff cloth were covered in goose bumps.

Nearly everyone had left before Peter stepped up to her. He didn't try to shake her hand, but came a little closer, running his fingers through his damp hair. "Kind of wet out," he said.

"Yeah." Molly stared into his dark eyes. She wanted to tell him about the gravestone, how the words were all wrong, how it was all a mistake. She needed to tell someone her dad was alive, especially here. Especially now. Would he understand if she . . .

"Peter?" called Mr. Birmingham. "Time for us to go."

"Just a minute, Dad." He cleared his throat. "I've gotta head back to Stony Brook tomorrow, Molly. Wish I could—"

"Come on, son," called Mr. Birmingham impatiently.

Peter tightened his jaw. "Sorry, Molly. Sorry about . . . about everything." He walked toward his family, then turned and took one last look at her before disappearing over the hill.

Late that night, Molly lay in bed and listened. The sobs coming from Mom's room earlier in the evening had finally stopped. Molly closed her eyes and tried to picture her dad's face again. Nothing. She shut her eyes tighter, trying to imagine Dad laughing, Dad looking serious as he read the paper. She couldn't see him. His face was gone. The words on the gravestone had taken him from her.

She slipped out of bed, hesitated a moment, then grabbed the black dress from the closet and tiptoed downstairs. In the front hall she put on her dad's heavy wool coat, then went outside to the toolshed.

A soft September rain pattered against the tin roof as Molly felt her way into the shed. A rake, a hoe: She touched each tool in turn till she found the familiar thick wooden handle of the shovel.

With the dress bunched up against her chest and the heavy shovel resting on her shoulder, Molly crossed the deserted street, passed Birmingham's department store, Dee's Antiques, and the post office. She turned up Quincy Avenue, the town so quiet in the dark she could hear the flag on the town hall lawn, flapping in the wind. Reaching St. Luke's, she skirted the old wood building and climbed the grassy hill to the graveyard.

At her father's gravestone, Molly tossed the dress

to the ground, laid Mom's roses beside the black fabric, and started to work. With the town in blackout, the moon became her solitary work lamp. She plunged the shovel into the muddy earth in front of her dad's gravestone. There was no body in this ground. Just dirt, roots, and worms. Working her muscles, she lifted shovelful after shovelful and dumped the wet soil into a pile.

When the hole was deep enough, she tossed in the dress and buried it. Laying the shovel on the ground by the roses, she knelt and patted down the earth with her bare hands. Mud seeped between her fingers as she worked. Through wet bangs, Molly read the words carved into the granite. DECEMBER 2, 1911–AUGUST 18, 1944.

Heart pounding, muscles tensing, she pushed mud into the date of death and pressed it in with her thumb. DIED BRAVELY IN THE SERVICE OF HIS COUNTRY. She grabbed another handful of mud, feeling a sweet release as she filled each lying letter. In the rain. In the dark. Molly worked until there were only three words left on the stone.

GEORGE FOWLER . . . LIVES . . .

six

Predictions

Algebra. Molly's fingers ached as she completed the last problem, turned her paper over, and stared out the classroom window. It was late November. The giant maple on the hill across the road stood leafless, its bony twigs reaching into the mist. It had been two months since she'd buried the black dress. Mom had discovered the dress was missing and demanded to know where it was. Molly hadn't told her. She was grounded and given mountains of chores, but it had been worth it.

Mom and Grandma had taken Kevin to the graveyard every Sunday afternoon, but Molly hadn't gone back since that night. Autumn rains had probably washed her mud away from the stone long ago.

It was better to remember the gravestone just the way she'd left it, all those mud-filled letters revealing the truth hidden in the stone—GEORGE FOWLER LIVES.

"We've got just a few minutes before the last bell today to discuss war news," said Mrs. LaCasse. Molly turned in her math paper, wishing again that she went to a bigger school, where junior high kids actually changed classrooms when they studied different subjects.

"I've got some war news," said Sam.

"Yes, Sam. What is it?"

"Grandpa and I just got the telegram yesterday about my dad. The Japs wounded him in the Philippines, and he's a hero. When he gets out of the hospital, they're gonna send him home."

"I'm glad he'll be back with us soon. I'm sure you and your grandfather could use the help at Henson's Market."

Sam jammed his hands in his jean pockets. "Won't be home right away, Mrs. LaCasse. He lost his right leg from the knee down. Has to stay in the hospital a couple more months."

"We're sorry to hear that, Sam," said Mrs. La-Casse.

"If I could get my hands on the Jap who—"

"That's enough, Sam! You may sit down."

Sam shot a fiery look at Jane, the vein on the side of his neck throbbing.

Mrs. LaCasse crossed her arms and narrowed her eyes. "I said you may sit down."

Sam sat and hunched over his desk.

Robbie raised his hand.

"Yes?"

"My dad says he saw some guys building a big fence around the old Civilian Conservation Corps camp outside of town."

"What's this got to do with war news, Robbie?"

"Well, my dad says the lumber mill can't get enough loggers to cut trees for pulpwood right now, 'cause of the war."

"Yes, that's true," said Mrs. LaCasse.

"He says they're puttin' up that fence so they can bring POWs in there. Germans or maybe Japs."

"That's Japanese, Robbie."

"Yeah, well, you know, since they've been rounding up the Japs, uh, Japanese, from the big cities the last couple of years and sending them off to internment camps. My dad says they oughta bring some out here and put them to work logging timber 'cause—"

"This is all conjecture, Robbie. I'm sure there's another perfectly good explanation for that fence," said Mrs. LaCasse. But no one was listening. Every eye was fixed on Jane, who stared straight ahead, unblinking, her face an unreadable mask.

"But my dad thinks—"

"Thank you, Robbie. That's enough."

Molly watched Jane's chest rise and fall in short, quick breaths—the way a small animal breathes when it's afraid. She wanted to reach out to her, calm her, but she kept her hands clamped in her lap.

The afternoon bell rang. Binders slammed shut.

"We'll have to continue this another time. Don't forget to check the homework board before you leave. No excuses on late assignments. Class dismissed."

Kids grabbed their books, threw on their coats, and poured onto the playground.

"Hey, did ya hear that?" Sam called after Jane. "They're buildin' a camp for you and the rest of the Japs right outside of town!"

Jane took off running. Molly watched her race across the road, her black hair streaming out behind her as she ran.

The boys turned toward Cleveland Street. "What are you starin' at, Foul Breath?" called Sam. Molly blushed and looked away as Jane disappeared into the mist. She could still hear the boys laughing as she cut across the street and headed for the path that led down to the beach.

Fog rolled up from the water. Molly buttoned her sweater and followed a green zigzag of seaweed to the water's edge. Three seagulls landed and fought over a rotting fish tangled in the seaweed. Molly shivered, slipped her hands into her pocket, and wrapped her fingers around Peter's tin angel.

She gazed down the beach. A mile down the shore, shrouded in fog, was Keenan Cliff. At the base of the path leading up to the cliff was the place where she and Peter had stood by his fire. That was before the telegram. Before everything had changed. She remembered how certain she'd been that day that her dad would be home for Christmas. And Peter's gift had seemed like a sign. The memory stung.

Molly rubbed the tip of the tin wing. It warmed in her hand. If Dad had been hiding out, trying to make his way back to Allied territory, they may hear from him soon. Christmas hadn't come yet. There was still time.

She longed to walk the pebble beach all the way to Keenan Cliff, climb the steep path to the top, sit on the edge of the world, and look out to sea. But she couldn't take the time today. She was expected home to help in Mom's salon.

The gulls took off as she stepped over the fish skeleton. Walking against the singing wind, she'd just stopped to examine a shell when Mrs. Larkin came around the jutting rocks.

"What've you got there, Molly May?"

Molly looked up, startled. "What? Oh, a moon-snail shell."

"Oh, yes," said Mrs. Larkin. "Pretty things." She poked a pile of ribbon kelp with her walking stick. Tiny black flies swarmed out. Then she lifted her eyes to the horizon, a wisp of gray hair blowing across her cheek. "He'll come back," she said.

A shiver raced up Molly's spine. How did Mrs. Larkin know her dad would . . . or was she talking about her husband, Daniel, who was lost at sea?

Molly looked into Mrs. Larkin's light blue eyes. They were unreadable, like little tide pools swimming with alien life.

"Grandma?" Jane stepped around the boulders, a small pile of shells balanced on her schoolbooks. Seeing Molly, she stopped suddenly. "Oh," she said. A periwinkle shell fell from her history book, landing near a small green cluster of glasswort.

"Here's my girl," said Mrs. Larkin. Jane blushed. She picked up the periwinkle shell, took her grandmother's hand, and turned to go.

"Jane?"

Jane looked back.

"I hate the way Sam and Robbie and the rest of the kids . . . I mean, I don't think you have to worry about that stupid fence."

Jane's face lit up with a smile. Her shoulders eased.

"What fence?" asked Mrs. Larkin.

"Just some old fence," said Jane.

"Yeah," said Molly, "some old fence."

Now they were both smiling.

"Well, we'd best be getting on," said Mrs. Larkin. "I hear the kettle calling."

"You and your tea," said Jane.

"Me and my tea," laughed Mrs. Larkin.

Molly watched them weave along the shore, avoiding scattered rocks and driftwood, Jane stooping here and there to pick up a shell.

"He'll come back." That was what Mrs. Larkin had said. But she must have meant Mr. Larkin. She still thought he'd find his way home to her someday. Five years, and she was still waiting. How long would she hold on?

Jane and her grandmother had melted into the fog like wandering ghosts. Molly turned and tossed her moon-snail shell into the pounding waves. White water swirled, swallowing the shell.

seven

The Photograph

December had come and gone. Christmas without a word from Dad. January 1945, February, now it was nearly April. Still no word.

Molly jammed her hand into her sweater pocket and clasped Peter's angel as the class walked two by two down Quincy Avenue on the way to Keenan Library. They crossed the street passing the cherry trees that edged the town hall lawn. New leaves were sprouting from the gray twigs. Molly was glad to see this small, green promise of spring.

It had been a hard winter. She'd kept Dad in her heart through the cold, the dark, the endless snow spiraling down from the pewter sky. She'd stared at his photograph on the mantel until she'd memorized every detail of the picture: his strong chin, his easy smile. But the long wait had made her feel brittle and alone.

The only time she'd felt hopeful was when the family sat around the radio on Sunday nights and listened to President Roosevelt's "Fireside Chats." One evening when the snow was piling up against the house, Mr. Roosevelt had said, "We are going forward on a long, rough road—and in all journeys, the last miles are the hardest." Molly had felt like he was right beside her then, encouraging her along, telling her not to give up on her father.

A few days later she told her mom how the broadcast had given her hope about Dad. Big mistake. Mom had turned pale and called Reverend Olson. He'd come over to comfort Molly and talk about her father's death. Together, they'd prayed for her father's soul. Reverend Olson praying for a dead man. Molly praying for a live one. After several visits, Reverend Olson had left, telling her mom Molly was better, that she'd come to accept the truth about her father. Molly wasn't sure how he'd arrived at this understanding, but she was glad to see him go.

The class followed Mrs. LaCasse around the corner past Principal Wierman's house. The wash line in the backyard sported three white T-shirts and a pair of boxers. Molly blushed and looked away.

"Hey, Robbie," Sam called from his place in line. "Remember that fence your dad was telling you about at the old CCC camp?"

"Yeah."

"Well, my dad drove past it the other day on his way to Gainsville. Said he saw some army trucks parked up there."

Molly tried not to listen. Ever since Sam's dad had come home, it was, "My dad says this and my dad says that."

"My dad said they've built a guard tower up there, too," added Sam. He turned to flash a white-toothed grin at Jane. "Looks like they'll be bringing POWs in for sure." Sam wiggled his brows at Molly. "You gonna visit your buddy when she's in the internment camp?"

"Lay off, Sam," said Molly, feeling a warm blush wash up her cheeks as she stared straight ahead. With every step she willed Sam to disappear or, better yet, explode, leaving only a small trail of smoke behind.

Up the road was the old two-story library building, gaps of gray wood showing where the blue paint had worn away. Above the sagging steps, an American flag fluttered between two dusty windows.

When they entered the library, the class dispersed into row upon row of shelves. Molly slipped into a vacant nonfiction aisle and walked between the towering shelves. She ran a finger along the rough book bindings in the history section till she came to a title that made her stop and look again. It read simply, *View from the Shore: A History of Keenan Maine*. Molly pulled the volume from the shelf. She was still flipping the pages showing old photographs of Maine lobstermen standing beside their stacks of lobster traps when Peter stepped around the shelves, loaded down with books.

"Hey, Molly."

"Hey, Peter. What are you doing in town?"

"Two-week spring break. I don't usually come home for Easter, but"—He shifted his book stack—"Don't you get Easter off?"

"Yeah, but our vacation starts next week."

"Oh," said Peter. He looked at the floor, shuffled his feet. Molly scanned the book bindings in Peter's stack. All of them had the word "airplane" in the title. He looked up from the floor, and she pretended a sudden interest in her own book. Turning the page, she found a photograph of St. George's Church. A two-page spread. Her breath quickened as she looked closer. The photo had been taken before the landslide. It showed a stained-glass window, *her* stained-glass window. "Oh," she said aloud, then clamped her lips shut as Peter stepped closer.

"What've you got?" he asked.

"A photograph."

"St. George's," he said, then leaned back to regrip his heavy load. "Wow, look at that stained-glass window."

She *had* been looking at the window and it was sending chills across the back of her neck. The stained glass showed St. George in full armor, spear and shield held high to battle the dragon.

The photo had finally solved the mystery of the strange eye she'd found. It was the eye of the dragon.

"Peter? This window . . ." She pointed to the dragon, her hand feeling suddenly cold as she touched the glass fire spewing from the dragon's jaws.

Peter leaned in. She could feel his breath on her neck.

Sally Pratt came around the corner and peered over Molly's shoulder. Molly pulled away, slamming the book shut.

"Come on," Sally said. "Mrs. LaCasse sent me to look for stragglers. We're supposed to meet Mrs. Lemieux upstairs for her lecture on coastal birds."

"I already know about coastal birds."

Sally crossed her arms. "Well, you're supposed to come, anyway." She leaned against the shelf and gave Peter a smile. "Hey, Peter."

"Hey."

"All right," said Molly, taking Sally by the elbow. "Guess we'd better go."

Peter flashed Molly an intense look before she left the nonfiction aisle with Sally.

"Are you sweet on Peter Birmingham?" asked Sally as they headed up the stairs.

"What? No. I'm not sweet on anybody, and don't you start any rumors, Sally."

Sally squinted in the dusty sunlight filtering through the stairway window. It was useless telling her not to spread stories. Sally was a talker.

Mrs. Lemieux was deep into her lecture on the mating habits of osprey, when they reached the conference room. Molly slipped into a chair, carefully opened her book under the table, and took another peek at the old photograph. It had been a beautiful window. She would have loved to have gone to a Sunday service in a church with a window like that. No matter how boring the sermon was, she could have still looked at St. George, spear and shield in hand, battling the dragon.

Later that afternoon, Molly pulled the box of stained glass out from under her bed and lifted a small piece up to the light. Part of a man's face. It wasn't Adam, as she'd supposed for so many months, but St. George. She placed the piece on the bed next to the library book. Now that she had the photograph, she could re-create the stained-glass window. At least she could try. And if Dad escaped—no, *when* he escaped—she'd give it to him just like she'd planned.

Slipping into the hall, she paused at the top of the landing and listened. Laughter downstairs. Strange. Grandma was out, and Mom didn't usually let her customers into the kitchen. Molly waited. More laughter. She hadn't heard Mom laugh like that in months. She thought of going down to see who it was, but she turned instead and headed up the narrow attic stairs.

Dust flew as she searched the darkened walls for the old wood-framed window. Finding it in the cobwebbed corner, she pulled the large, four-foot-square window away from its resting place. It had been leaning up against the wall for years, waiting to be fixed.

Kneeling down to inspect the glass, she traced a small crack running diagonally along the bottom corner with the tip of her finger. She'd have to use extra glue there. Molly picked up the heavy window, staggered down the narrow stairs, and carefully lowered it onto the rag rug by her bed.

Her breathing shallowed as her excitement grew. Yes, she'd glue the pieces down and make a new stained-glass window for her dad. The book said the original had been five by five. Her window would be smaller. She'd have to leave out most of the blue glass sky to fit the dragon in, but when her dad saw the light pouring through St. George's armor, he'd put his arm around her and smile. She hugged herself, then headed down to the kitchen for the window cleaner.

Laughter again. Someone was definitely in the kitchen with Mom. Molly paused to listen. This time the laughter was deep, sprinkled occasionally with Mom's giggles. She pushed open the door.

Sam's dad was sitting at the kitchen table.

"Oh, Molly," said Mom, nervously hopping to a stand. "You remember Mr. Henson from Henson's Market?"

Molly held the doorknob, her tongue suddenly thick as driftwood. Of course she knew Sam's dad. She'd shopped at Henson's Market thousands of times. And she knew he was back from the war. Sam had been talking about it all week. Still, she was surprised to see him in her kitchen.

Mr. Henson leaned back in his chair. He was dressed in full uniform. Sitting there, Molly couldn't tell which leg was false. She steered her eyes away from his feet.

"Say hello, Molly," urged Mom.

"Hello." Molly stepped in and shut the door.

"You're so tall," said Mr. Henson. "My Sam's grown up, too." He turned to Molly's mom. "I think working at the market with his grandpa has helped mature the boy." He shook his head. "I couldn't believe my eyes when I stepped off the train. It was like looking in the mirror." He glanced at his stiff leg. "Well, looking in the mirror a very long time ago."

"Not so long ago," said Mom.

Molly watched a wine-colored blush spread up Mr. Henson's neck. He took out a cigarette and lit up.

"Mom, don't you have any customers coming?"

"Mrs. Fitzhenry will be here at four o'clock, dear. You'll remember to come sweep up after she's gone, won't you?"

Molly crossed the kitchen, ignoring the question. Why was her mom asking her that? She'd been sweeping up after the last customer of the day for years. Mom hummed as she poured coffee into a mug and passed it to Mr. Henson.

Dad's mug. Molly bit her lip as she grabbed a rag and a bottle of window cleaner from the pantry.

"Cleaning your room, dear?" asked Mom, staring at the rag in Molly's hand.

"Yes," lied Molly.

"Good girl."

Molly rushed through the hall, up the stairs, and closed her door. She hadn't seen a man in the kitchen since Dad had left for the war. But Sam's dad was down there right now, sprawling across the kitchen chair, relaxing peacefully as if it were his own kitchen. She gripped the rag and closed her eyes, wishing him out of his chair, out of her kitchen, down the street, back to his store.

Kneeling on her rug, she sprayed the dusty window, her own shadowed face staring back at her as she wiped the glass.

"Don't be sad," Dad had said that day on the cliff. Then he'd given her the watch chain. "Our time together has to stop for a while, Molly," he'd said.

She dried the window with her soft white cloth. Time stopping. She wished it had. Time had kept right on going: Thanksgiving, the first snow of the year, Christmas, all without Dad. Now it was spring, leaves were sprouting on the apple tree out back, still Dad hadn't come home, and people like Mr. Henson were coming over, sitting at the kitchen table, drinking coffee from Dad's favorite mug. Well, thought Molly as she tugged the box of stained glass toward her, if Mom didn't have any better sense than to give Dad's mug to an ordinary visitor, she'd just have to hide it.

She fingered through the glass, wondering where to start. That day on the cliff, Dad had turned the watch over. Showed her the secret place at the back. "You could send me the watch with a note if you get in trouble," she'd told him. And Dad had smiled. "It would have to be a pretty short message, little bird."

She didn't care if the message were short, at least if he sent the watch, she'd know he was alive. Why hadn't he sent it to her? She wrapped her fingers around a piece of green glass till she felt the sharp edges poking into her palm. Maybe he'd been captured and was in a German prison camp. He'd wanted to send the watch, but hadn't been able to get it past the guards yet.

Slowly, she opened her hand. Yes, that was it. He hadn't been able to get it past the guards. But Dad was smart. Very smart. He'd find a way.

Molly stood and went to her window, overlooking her backyard and farther out, the sea. She opened the window and smelled the salty air. A gentle rain was falling. Drops clung to the new green leaves on her apple tree. Send a message to me, she thought. You have to escape. Come home soon. We need you because . . .

Her heart swelled . . . because we all need you and Mr. Henson is in our kitchen. She looked to the far horizon, willing the words out to sea, over to Germany, through the barbed-wire fence to her dad.

Wind swept a spray of raindrops across her cheek, she closed the window, and went back to her work, picking out all the green pieces one by one. Dragon scales.

The radio played downstairs, but laughter was no longer coming from the kitchen. She wasn't sure if that was a good thing or a bad thing.

Molly carefully placed the green glass on the window and began to build a dragon.

Dee's News

The next day, Molly sat at the kitchen table stirring a spoonful of sugar into her tea. She took a sip, letting the bittersweet flavor nip the edges of her tongue. She'd taken the long way home, hoping to run into Peter on the beach, but there was no sign of him by the climbing rocks or at the base of Keenan Cliff. She'd waited in the shelter of the rocks, water swirling into the tide pools, a sharp salt wind stinging her cheeks. After an hour, she'd given up and gone home.

Grandma came in from the garden. "Bit nippy outside," she said, pulling off her dirt-stained gloves. She looked around the kitchen. "Where's Kevin?"

"Don't know."

Grandma washed her hands. "Well, I expect he'll be along soon."

"He'd better be," said Molly. "He's got chores." She finished her tea, cleaned her cup, and placed it in the cupboard. The phone rang.

"Oh, hello, Charlotte," said Grandma.

While Grandma chatted on the phone, Molly took her dad's mug from the shelf, peered inside, and frowned. There was a dark brown coffee ring on the bottom. Mom hadn't done a very good job of washing up after Mr. Henson yesterday. Molly grabbed the sponge and scrubbed it fiercely till the white soap bubbles cleaned away all traces of Mr. Henson. Rinsing it with scalding water, she dried the mug and shoved it into the depths of the pantry behind an ancient bag of dried beans. Safe.

Grandma hung up and turned around. "It's after four. Better be getting on down to give your mom a hand, Molly."

"Yeah, I know." Molly crossed the room and opened the door halfway. "Who's she got down there this afternoon?"

"Dee Brown."

"Oh, Jeeze, not Dee."

"The old bird herself," said Grandma.

Molly trailed down the narrow steps. The smell of hair spray assailed her nose as she stepped into the salon.

"There you are, dear. I need you to sweep up."

Molly grabbed the broom from the utility closet

and began to sweep the clumps of bleached-blonde hair into a neat pile.

"Dee has a big date tonight. Don't you, Dee?" said Mom.

"Aw, now stop making more of it than it is," chuckled Dee.

"She's going out with Mr. Standish, from Gainsville," Mom said as she deftly unrolled a strand of hair and tossed the last curler into the basin.

Molly flicked on the radio. The Andrews Sisters sang, "Don't sit under the apple tree with anyone else but me." She leaned against the broom handle and stared out the window at the apple tree in the back-yard. On summer nights, Dad used to push her on the swing. Higher. Higher. Till she thought she'd fly off the edge of the world.

"I suppose you've heard about the POWs," said Dee.

"Of course. The hairdresser is always the first to hear everything."

Molly turned off the radio. "POWs?"

"Yes! POWs," said Dee. "The Gainsville Lumber Mill needs more fir trees cut for pulpwood. The log-gers having gone off to war and all. They've brought a trainload of Germans over from a prison camp to log the timber in the hills just outside of town."

"Germans," whispered Molly. Her face cast a pale reflection in the beauty shop mirror. Sam had been right. They *were* bringing POWs in. But Germans. Not Japanese. "Are you sure it was Germans?"

"Sure?" said Dee. "Of course I'm sure. My sister,

Louise, saw them changing trains in Gainsville. Said they marched along like soldiers, only they had the letters 'PW' on their backs."

Dee laughed. "Bunch of hoboes jumped outta their boxcars and ran for their lives when they saw them coming. My sister said you should've seen those hoboes skedaddle into the woods."

"Where will they be putting the POWs up?" asked Mom.

"I've heard they'll be staying at the CCC camp," said Dee. "They've built a big fence and they'll have guards and all, but it's not safe." She clicked her tongue in warning. "I mean the children and all. Being so close to the enemy. What if one escapes and takes one of us prisoner?"

Molly gripped the broom handle tighter.

"No one's going to escape, Dee," said Mom. "Now keep still, or your hairdo will be spoiled."

Dee took a final look in the mirror.

"Like it?" asked Mom, slipping off the apron.

Dee swung around in her chair. "Gail, you're a genius!" She stood and brushed the wrinkles out of her dress, then slipped a penny into Molly's hand. "Buy yourself a treat, sugar," Dee said with a wink, then trotted out the door.

Mom hung out the "closed" sign, sat down, removed her high heels, and rubbed her ankles. "Where's Kevin?"

Molly stashed the broom. "Don't know."

"You'd better mop the floor then," Mom said, sighing.

"I won't. That's Kevin's job."

Mom's pale skin stretched across her bony cheeks as she frowned. "All right," she said, glancing at the mop in the corner. "Then go find him, Molly. This floor has to be cleaned before dinner."

Molly raced up the stairs, threw on her sweater, and rushed out the kitchen door to the back steps. Kevin would probably be somewhere on the beach climbing on the boulders. She kicked a rock down the steps, *clickity, clickity, clickity,* cupped her hands to her mouth, and called, "Kevin!"

No answer.

Molly walked down steps, headed across the beach, and searched the base of the climbing rocks for Kevin. Overhead a flock of snow geese cut through the clouds on their way to the marshlands beyond Keenan Harbor.

The crunching sound of horse hoofs on the pebble beach made her turn suddenly. Peter pulled his chestnut brown horse to a halt, leaned forward, and smiled a crooked smile. "Hey, Molly. What's up?"

"Nothing. I just came down here to look for my little brother."

"He's not here," said Peter. "Saw him half an hour ago heading up the old logging road with a couple of other kids."

"The POWs," said Molly.

"What POWs?"

"Germans," said Molly, heart racing. "Might just be a rumor, but people are saying they've brought them here to do some logging. My brother must have gone up to see."

"Hop on," said Peter, pulling his foot out of the stirrup. Molly took a hesitant step forward. She hadn't ridden a horse since she was eight years old.

"What's his name?"

"Blaze. Come on up. He won't hurt you."

Molly slid her shoe into the metal stirrup, took Peter's hand, and threw her leg over the saddle.

"Grab my waist!" shouted Peter as he gave Blaze a kick. Molly bounced awkwardly on the saddle as Blaze trotted along the shore and turned onto the dirt road that led to the woods.

Sea oats dipped in the wind, catching the honey-colored light as Blaze cleared the hilltop and galloped down the other side. Snow gone, the hills were awakening. Wild iris and forget-me-nots were scattered in the blowing grass, and along the rotting fence were clusters of fireweed and wild mustard. Molly wrapped her arms tighter around Peter's waist, sunlight soaking into her back and sliding down her spine.

Two miles up the dirt road, they came to a halt when they spotted a line of army trucks parked beside a ditch. Peter steered Blaze into the forest, and helped Molly down from the saddle.

"Listen," he whispered as he tied Blaze's reins to a nearby tree. Through the thick woods, Molly heard the rhythmic sound of saws. *Zuuza! Zuuza!* Peter crouched low and headed in the direction of the sound. The railroad track cut a straight path

71

through the dark woods. Just across the track where the tree line resumed, Molly spotted a U. S. Army guard leaning against a fir tree. He lit a cigarette, tilted his head back and exhaled a slow stream of smoke.

Zuuza! Zuuza! In the distance Molly saw two sweat-soaked backs. Each gray shirt bore the letters "PW." Her hands went suddenly cold. There they were. The Nazis. Five of them. There were probably more POWs spread around in the woods with U. S. soldiers guarding them. But these five were close. So close, she could hear one of them grunting with exertion as he pushed and pulled the saw.

Spotting an old wood cabin on this side of the tracks, they darted from tree to tree. Looking first left, then right, Molly ran to the side wall of the cabin, slipped around the corner, and stepped across the doorway. Suddenly two arms thrust out of the dark and grabbed her. A dirty hand clamped over her mouth.

White-hot fear spilled through her limbs, melting her knees into putty. She was caught by a Nazi! Where would he take her? Would he kill her? Peter came around the corner and grabbed her attacker. "Let go of her, Sam!"

Relief spread through Molly's veins, followed by a rush of anger. She bit Sam's sweaty finger. "Ouch!" he yelped, jumping back and violently shaking his hand.

"Shh!" hissed the rest of the kids inside the cabin. Kevin poked his head out of the doorway, smiled, and shoved his hands into his pockets. Molly ran her eye along his tangled blond head, his freckled face, and rumpled striped shirt. She wanted to hit him. She wanted to hug him. Confusion swept hot prickles down her arms.

"What are you doin' here, Birmingham?" said Sam, spitting the word "Birmingham" out like poison.

"The same thing you are."

Sam breathed heavily. "Okay, but you'd better not screw up our plans." He stepped inside and pulled a BB gun from the darkened corner.

A cold panic rushed up Molly's back.

"One of them's comin' closer," said Robbie.

Sam rushed to the far wall and poked his BB gun out the broken window.

"What in the hell are you doing?" cried Peter. He dove for the gun, but Robbie leaped out of the shadows, catching him in a neckhold.

At that same moment, Joe grabbed Molly's hair, yanked her head back, and covered her mouth with his hand. Smells of dirt and bicycle grease filled her nose.

The POW across the tracks laid down his ax and wiped his damp forehead.

"I'm gonna teach that Nazi a lesson," Sam said between clenched teeth. The tendon on the back of his hand twitched as he wiggled his trigger finger.

"Those Germans killed my dad!" said Kevin, grabbing Sam's shirt. "Kill him for me, Sam!"

Sam put his free arm around Kevin. "I'll get him, little guy. Just watch me."

Molly struggled against Joe's armhold as Sam eye-balled the enemy along the barrel of his BB gun and pulled the trigger. *Bang!* A BB whizzed past the POW's baggy trousers. He jumped and slapped his leg.

"He thought it was a bee," giggled Kevin.

"Some bee," said Sam. "I'll show that Nazi how this bee can sting!" He shot again. *Ping!* The BB hit the railroad tracks. "Damn!"

The sandy-haired POW spun around and stared at the cabin.

Sam shot a third time. *Bang!* The BB grazed the man's face. "Oof!" He pressed his hand to his bloody cheek and began to march toward the cabin.

"I got you, you Nazi bastard!" called Sam, waving his gun in the air. "I got you good!"

As the POW stumbled toward them, everything seemed to switch to slow motion. White grass waved around his black shoes. Wind rippled his large, gray shirt as he crossed the railroad tracks.

"Halt!" Two army guards suddenly appeared from the dense forest. One raised his rifle to the sky and fired a warning shot. The German fell, a pocket watch dropping onto the rocky ground be-side his knee. Molly's heart caught in her throat as she squinted through the broken window. The pocket watch had no chain, just some string, and there was a letter engraved on the cover. The POW quickly stuffed it back into his pants as two guards rushed forward, pointing their rifle barrels at his back.

Sam ducked under the window.

"Get up," ordered the guard. The POW stood, hands above his head, blood streaming down his cheek.

"*Kinder! Kinder!*" he puffed, motioning to the shack. The GI turned toward the cabin, peered inside, and raised his rifle.

"If you kids aren't outta here in three minutes, I'll throw your butts in jail!" he shouted.

Everyone scattered. Sam, Robbie, and Joe dove for their bicycles. Molly ran after Peter. They cut through the trees on the far side of the tracks and climbed into the saddle. "Hold on!" shouted Peter.

"Wait! Where's Kevin?" Molly panted.

"Over there!" Peter pointed to the grassy hill across the logging road. Kevin was running down the hill at top speed, his blond head bobbing up and down in the tall grass.

"Home?" shouted Peter.

"No! I can't!" cried Molly.

"Where, then?"

Molly couldn't answer. She licked her lips, tasting the waxy flavor of bicycle grease as Blaze galloped down the dirt road.

A rush of wind cooled her burning face. She leaned aside, feeling the sting of salt as the sweat on her cheeks dried. Her dad's watch. It had to be. She couldn't have been wrong. It was gold, had no watch chain, and it had the letter "F" engraved on the cover. It was the sign she'd prayed for. Dad must have found a way to send the watch to her.

She held on to Peter's waist and laid her cheek on his shoulder. The earth whirled beneath Blaze's hoofs. Clouds of dust engulfing them. She wanted Peter to ride through the hills and up the steep path to Keenan Cliff. Ride to the edge of the world.

nine

Cliff Edge

Blaze raced up the path and came to a halt at St. George's Ruin.

"Good boy," whispered Peter, giving his neck a pat. He dismounted and held out his hand. Molly sat motionless, staring into Peter's dark brown eyes. How had Peter known she wanted to come here?

"What's wrong, Molly?"

"Nothing." She took his hand and slid down from the saddle. Blaze nibbled on the dry grass as Peter looped his reins around a spruce branch.

"Want to go to the edge?"

Molly nodded. Walking as close as they dared, they lay down and looked over the cliff. Waves crashed far below, quilting into blue-green patches as they pulled away from shore.

"Tide's in," said Peter. "Can't see the stone cross too well today."

"I used to come up here all the time with my dad," said Molly.

Peter frowned. "You're lucky. My dad's too busy with his stupid chain of department stores to do anything like that."

Molly winced and stared at her fingernails. Each one had a thin line of dirt beneath. "Why don't you ask him to spend some time with you?"

"Wouldn't listen. Work's more important."

"But he's your dad."

"So?"

"If my dad were here I'd—"

"Look. You love your dad. It's not the same for me, okay, so just drop it!"

But Molly couldn't drop it. Peter hadn't said, "You *loved* your dad." He'd said, "You *love* your dad." Here. Now. In the present tense. And the crazy secret spilled out of Molly's mouth before she could catch it.

"My dad's alive," she breathed. "I know he is. Everyone in town thinks he's dead because of that stupid telegram. But the telegram could have been wrong. He might have bailed out and been captured." She nearly faltered when she caught Peter's astonished expression, but the words were erupting from somewhere deep in her chest. It felt so good to say them aloud.

"I burned that stupid telegram. I'd know if my dad were dead. We had this . . . this . . . I can't explain, but I knew what he was thinking sometimes, or he'd know what I was thinking. Like I'd be thinking I wanted to come up here and look at the cross, and he'd just say, 'Come on, Molly.' I'd follow him, wondering if he'd take me where I wanted go, and he would! He'd come right up here, just like you did today."

She stopped. Oh! she'd let that slip out. She hadn't meant to tell Peter she'd wanted to come here.

"It's where I wanted to come, too," said Peter.

Molly rested her chin in her palms and spread her fingers across her face to cover the blush that burned her cheeks. "Look," she said. The sea pulled back, exposing the stone cross beneath. Then crash, the cross was gone.

Peter tossed a rock. It clattered down the side of the cliff and fell into the sea. An uneasy silence built between them like a wave that wouldn't break.

"I . . . I saw something today," Molly said finally. "That German POW. He had something. Something of my dad's, I think."

"How could a POW have something of your dad's?"

"I don't know, but I saw it. I swear I saw my dad's pocket watch."

"Lots of people have pocket watches."

"My dad's watch is different. It's got his initial 'F' engraved on the cover. I saw the 'F.' And the watch didn't have a chain, just some string."

Peter stared at Molly, cloud shadows playing now light, now dark, patterns on his face. His eyebrows curved downward with interest, or disbelief; Molly couldn't tell which.

"Before Dad left, he took the chain off his pocket watch and gave it to me."

"Why?"

Molly felt the heat of irritation prickling her skin. She wasn't going to tell him what her dad had said when he'd given her the chain. It was private.

"The thing is, there's a double back on the watch. A secret place to put photographs or messages. I asked him to send the watch to me if he was in trouble."

"And you think he gave the watch to the POW?"

"Not gave it to him exactly."

"Even if the watch did get into German hands after the plane crash . . . the likelihood of it ending up here. I mean ending up with a POW in Keenan . . ." He stared at the churning water below.

Molly shifted her weight, feeling the small, hard rocks scratch against her hipbones. Now that the story was out, she felt stupid. The whole thing sounded crazy. Her muscles tensed. She wanted to jump up and run away from Peter. He'd probably use the story against her. Tell people she was crazy. Then kids would spread it all over the school: "Molly thinks her dad's still alive. Can you believe it? She thinks a POW has her father's watch. Next she'll be lighting beacon fires on Keenan Cliff the way Mrs. Larkin used to do."

"I guess we could check it out," said Peter.

Molly shook the voices from her head. "What?"

"The watch. I've got nothing else to do this spring break. But we'd have to figure out a way to get it from the POW."

A slow smile spread across Molly's face. "You mean you believe me?"

Peter frowned. "I can't imagine how it could have happened, but you saw something. We might as well take a look, if only to settle things in your own mind."

The sun was slipping down behind the mountains, spilling gold across the clouds and sea. Peter would help her get the watch. Molly felt like a thief stealing sudden joy from the sun, the sea. No one could make her give it back.

They scooted away from the cliff. Peter plucked a handful of grass for Blaze as Molly brushed off her pants. How would they meet with the POW? If they got close enough, how could they tell him that she needed the watch? He probably didn't even understand English.

"We'll need to write a note in German," Molly said at last. "Do they teach German at your school?"

"French."

"Oh."

Blaze nibbled on the grass in Peter's palm. "Don't worry. There must be someone in town who knows German."

"What about Mr. Mossel at your dad's store?" asked Molly.

"Nope, he's Jewish. He'd never agree to write

anything in German, even if he knew how. His sister and her family are still in Europe. Last he heard they were hoping to make their way to Sweden, but he hasn't gotten any word from her in nearly two years. He doesn't know if she's in hiding or in a concentration camp or . . . anyway," Peter said, "he was real upset about the German POWs coming to town."

Molly looked across the cliffs. "There's only one person I know of who knows German."

"Who?"

"Mrs. Larkin."

Peter rubbed Blaze's brown neck. "You mean the old lady who used to light those beacon fires on Keenan Cliff?"

"She wasn't always like that. She used to teach French and German to the seventh and eighth graders at our school."

"You think she could help us write a note?"

"Sure," said Molly with a shrug. She looked across the churning water, hoping Peter couldn't read the uncertainty in her face.

That night, Molly ran across the moonlit street and met Peter behind Birmingham's department store. They cut through the alley, followed the railroad tracks to Bradley Street, then headed up the steep hill toward the Larkins'.

Molly was worried about the note. She wasn't sure how she'd get Mrs. Larkin to agree to write it in German. Peter seemed absorbed in thought, too. He shoved his hands into his pockets and kicked a rock into the fireweed that grew in great green clumps along the side of the road. "Molly?"

"Yeah?"

"Are you sure it was your dad's watch you saw?"

"Yes. I already told you."

"How do you think that POW got ahold of it?"

"I'm not sure."

They continued up the steep hill, the town falling into the dark behind them. "Well," said Peter, "I've been thinking about it, and I've got an idea."

"Like what?" puffed Molly, picking up a small branch and tracing a crack in the road as she turned the corner. "Maybe the German found it on his body after the plane crash. I've heard soldiers loot bodies whenever they . . . "

Molly stopped, her skin suddenly cold. "Then the watch couldn't tell us if my dad were alive or . . ." Her teeth began to chatter, and she willed her jaw shut, turned to the ravine at the side of the road, and threw her stick over the edge. It clattered against an old rusty barrel someone had dumped there.

"I don't think that's what happened," she said.

Peter stooped down to tie his shoe. "You got any better ideas?"

"I don't know! Maybe my dad parachuted out of the plane just before it crashed. The telegram said no one saw a parachute, but if there were clouds in the way . . . anyway, he could have been captured by the Nazis after he landed. He might be in a German prison camp right now."

"So a Nazi guard took your dad's watch, got captured later, and ended up a POW?"

"Yeah."

Peter looked up at her, moonlight streaked across his face. "I still can't see how that Nazi would have ended up here in Keenan."

"Look," said Molly, digging her nails into her palms, "you don't have to come with me to the Larkins'. You can go home right now. I'll get the note and go after that POW myself!"

Peter ran his hand through his hair. "Hey, I was just trying to make some sense out of this stuff. I mean, haven't you been wondering about it yourself?"

She *had* been wondering about it. Somehow a German had her dad's watch. Up till now she'd thought it was proof her dad was still alive. But, now . . . She stared at the moon's face caught in a shallow puddle by her feet. The mouth drooped. The eyes were dark and hollow.

Peter stepped closer. "Sorry, Molly. I didn't mean to . . . " He shoved his hands in his pockets. "Anyway, we're sure to find out more once we get ahold of the watch."

They started up the road again, an uneasy truce between them, until they reached the top of the grade, where they stood facing a small, shabby house.

"This is it," said Molly, taking a quick look up and down the dark street. If Sam or any of the other kids saw her here . . . "Come on," she whispered, darting across the wiry grass.

"Creepy," said Peter. "You ever been here before?"

"What? No—never." She was going to say, "Nobody comes here," but checked herself, jailing the unsaid words against the back of her teeth.

"You think they'll invite us in?"

Molly let Peter's question hang in the air as they climbed the steps and knocked.

The door creaked open. Jane peeked out. "Molly?"

"Hi, Jane. Can . . . can we come in a minute?"

"What's happened?" gasped Jane. "Is Grandma all right? Is she hurt?"

"No," said Peter. "Your grandmother's fine. At least . . . I mean that's not why we're here."

Jane tilted her head. "Oh."

"Can we come in?" asked Peter.

She opened the door a bit wider. "I . . . I guess so." They stepped into the dark hall and followed Jane to the kitchen.

"Do you want tea or something? I'm just making some."

"Sure." Molly sat in a stiff high-back chair and looked around the kitchen. Peeling wallpaper, pink roses turned brown with age. The cabinets were open. No doors to hide the mismatched dishes neatly stacked inside.

A fat, gray cat jumped up from under the table and folded herself into her lap.

"Don't mind Muse," said Jane. "Just push her off if she gets to be too much for you."

85

Muse purred contentedly as Jane poured light green tea into each cup. Pretty soon Molly would have to tell her what they were doing there. Her tongue felt thick and heavy. She sensed Jane's eyes upon her as she stirred a small snowstorm of sugar into her cup, then licked the spoon, feeling suddenly embarrassed, not knowing where to lay it down.

"Do you know when your grandmother will be back from . . . " Molly paused. Mrs. Larkin was probably walking the beach, watching, waiting for her husband's boat.

Molly tried again. "We need your grandma to help us write a note."

"Why?" A thin cloud of steam rose from Jane's teacup, veiling the delicate features of her face.

Molly stroked Muse. "We saw the POWs. You know, the ones that are cutting trees for the lumber mill? One of the Germans has something I want."

"A pocket watch," Peter added.

"We need a note in German to . . ." Her words fell silent as she stared at Jane's hardened face.

Muse leaped to the floor as Jane stood up and backed toward the stove. "I thought you were different, Molly."

"What? What do you mean?"

"Sam put you up to this, didn't he?"

"Sam? No! He—"

"I'm not stupid! Sam told you to get my grandma to write a German note so he could tell everyone in town we're spies!" She grabbed a dish towel and twisted it around her hand. "Grandma would be sent to jail, and I'd be put in a Japanese internment camp. That's what Sam wants! It's what the whole town wants!"

Molly held up her hand. "No! Wait! Sam doesn't have anything to do with this. I swear it, Jane. I didn't want to tell you why I needed the note, because it's . . . personal.

"Really, Jane," said Peter, "you have to believe us. We're not here to get you in any trouble."

Jane frowned, unwound the dish towel, and looked intently at Molly. "What's this about?"

"The pocket watch I saw on the POW. I need to get ahold of it. I . . . I think it's my dad's. It might have a message inside for me."

"Why do you think it's your dad's?"

"I saw his initial on the cover."

Jane frowned, tilting her head.

"I know it sounds crazy," said Molly, "but I have to see it. I have to check it out."

Molly looked down at her hands, an awkward silence filling the room. Jane bit her lip, glanced over at Peter, then left the kitchen.

"Where's she going?" whispered Molly.

Peter shrugged and sloshed the tea around in his cup while they waited.

Molly was beginning to wonder if they should leave, when the kitchen door swung open, and Jane returned with a stack of German language books. She placed them on the table. "What do you want the note to say?" she asked, thumbing through the faded blue book on the top of the stack.

"I want to know where he got the pocket watch."

"You should ask if you can buy it from him," added Peter. "That way, you'll be able to check for a message in the back."

Jane flipped through the pages. "Where did you get your pocket watch," she mumbled.

In the dim light of the kitchen, they worked on the note together for over an hour, adding words, crossing them out, until the paper resembled a kindergartner's uncertain work.

"This is a mess," said Molly, rubbing her eraser across the paper. "And we don't even know if it's right."

Bang! The front door slammed. Muse leaped onto the table, scattering papers, as the squeaking sound of wet shoes headed toward the kitchen.

Mrs. Larkin opened the swinging door and stood in the pale light, her gray hair falling onto her sunken shoulders. "What's going on here?" she asked.

"Homework, Grandma," said Jane. "We're doing a foreign language assignment."

"I used to teach that," she said picking up the note. Her pale blue eyes scanned the page. "Doesn't make any sense," she said, dropping it back onto the table.

"We're supposed to translate this," said Jane, thrusting the English note into her grandmother's hand.

Mrs. Larkin clucked her tongue. "You were close." She grabbed the pencil and rewrote the sentences on the bottom of the page. "I would like to buy your pocket watch," she mumbled, turning to hang her coat on a hook by the door. She wiped a hunk of hair away from her face, then looked at Molly.

Molly's throat tightened as the old woman leaned toward her. "What are you after, Molly May?" she whispered.

Molly pressed her spine against the chair. "What? Nothing, I—"

"You're tired," said Jane sliding her arm around her grandmother's shoulder. "Come on upstairs to bed." She led her grandmother into the hall.

Molly stared at the door. "What did she mean by that?"

Peter scooted his chair closer. "Don't mind her." He put his hand on Molly's shoulder. "Let's just hope she knows enough German to have written us a good note."

Molly grabbed the piece of paper. Mrs. Larkin's handwriting looked like chicken scratches on the page. "I'll copy over the lettering," she said, grateful for the distraction.

As she printed out the note, Peter checked Mrs. Larkin's translation in the German dictionary. By the time Jane came back downstairs, they were done.

"Sorry about Grandma," said Jane as she saw them to the door.

"No big deal," said Peter. "She did a good job with the note."

"So," said Jane, "when are you gonna see the POW?"

Molly traced a crack along the porch with her sneaker. "Tomorrow afternoon, I guess."

"I'd like to come."

Peter eyed Molly, then looked at Jane. "It'll be dangerous."

Jane said nothing. She put her hands behind her back and waited.

"Four o'clock," said Peter. "The pasture gate behind my house."

For the first time that night, Jane smiled. "I'll be there," she said.

Gunfire

The next afternoon the three met in the far corner of Peter's pasture.

"Did you bring the money?" asked Molly.

"Got it," said Peter, handing it to Molly. "You think you can handle Tillie?"

"Sure," said Molly, looking at the brown mare uncertainly.

Peter nodded. "Jane can ride with me on Blaze. Tillie will follow along behind. She's pretty easy."

Molly gripped Tillie's reins as they trotted up the path. She hadn't ridden since she was eight, but she didn't want Peter to know that. By the time they turned onto the logging road, she began to feel more at ease in the saddle, moving in rhythm with her horse as they headed for the woods.

Two miles from Keenan they saw the line of army trucks parked along the edge of the logging road. Cutting into the trees, they dismounted and led the horses through the woods. Peter looped the reins around a low branch. "Ready, Molly?" he asked.

Molly clutched the note in her pocket. They could turn back now, forget the whole thing, but she heard herself saying, "Yeah, let's go."

They climbed through the dense forest, crouched behind the close-set firs, and gazed down the hill.

Zuuza. Zuuza. Two dark-haired POWs were sawing a fir tree below. The branches trembled in rhythm to the saw.

Molly pointed up the hill. Cutting a wide circle around the POWs, they climbed through the underbrush, hid behind a tangled raspberry bush, and looked down. The flesh pinpricked at the base of Molly's neck as she saw the man approaching a fallen tree below. It was the POW Sam had shot. She would recognize his large head and broad neck anywhere. His short hair was so blond, you could see the scalp beneath. The man leaned forward and chopped away the branches with his hatchet.

"Over there," warned Peter. At the far edge of the timberline, an army guard sat on a stump looking down the hill.

"We'll have to lure the POW out of sight," whispered Peter, pulling a pack of cigarettes from his shirt pocket.

"What are you doing?"

"Just watch." Peter crept a little closer and tossed

a cigarette down the hill onto the forest floor. They waited. Chop, chop, chop, the POW continued hacking away at the branches of the fallen tree.

"He doesn't see the cigarette," whispered Jane.

Peter waved his hand for her to be quiet, then pulled a second from the packet.

A ray of sun filtered through the trees, lighting up the German's blond hair. He straightened up and spotted the cigarette, then stood a moment, surveying the bushes suspiciously. The muscle of his jaw tightened as he looked now left, now right, then reached down and grabbed the cigarette from the forest floor.

Peter tossed another cigarette. The POW marched up the hill toward them. He stopped when his eyes caught Molly's. He peered at her, his gaze sharp as a sting. Molly covered her trembling mouth, trying to bite back the fear rising in her throat.

"Go on," whispered Peter. "He's out of the guard's sight. Now's your chance!" Molly took a deep breath and stepped out from behind the bushes.

Standing in the slanting sunlight, her legs softening into useless putty, she knew she was caught. She wouldn't be able to bend her rubbery knees and run from the towering man if she tried. Blood stampeded through her veins.

"Do . . . do you speak English?"

"*Kein Englisch,*" he said.

Molly tried to read the note. "*Woher hast du die Taschenuhr bekommen?* Where did you get your pocket watch?"

The POW raised his eyebrows in puzzlement. She fumbled through the next two sentences. The POW shook his head. He didn't understand her at all. Molly passed him the note and watched his light blue eyes dart back and forth along the crumpled paper as he read the words.

"Show him the money," called Peter. Molly dug into her pocket, pulled out two ten-dollar bills, and pushed them into the POW's broad hand.

The man's eyes widened. He laid down his hatchet and drew the watch from his pants pocket. Suddenly there were shouts from down below.

"Corporal! Where's the POW?"

"Get out of here, Molly!" called Peter. "They're on to us!"

Molly dove into the bush as two GIs rushed up the hill. The POW fled deeper into the woods. The GIs shouted, raised their rifles. The bushes exploded in gunfire, and the German fell.

Huddling next to Peter, her heart hammering in her throat, Molly watched the guards rush up the hill and over to the fallen man. Get up, thought Molly. You can't be hurt. Get up. But the POW didn't move.

The stocky GI planted the heel of his boot on the POW's shoulder and pushed him over onto his backside. Molly felt a rush of nausea. The German's face and chest were covered with blood.

"Crazy fool Nazis, always tryin' to escape! Come on, Corporal," he said, stooping down to check the body.

"Is he dead, sir?"

"He'll be dead soon if you don't get a move on!"

Molly couldn't breathe, couldn't even blink. Her eyes felt dry, her skin hard. Peter put his arm around her shoulder. She barely felt it.

As the GIs lifted the German, Molly's crumpled note drifted to the ground along with the money.

"Hey, what's this?" The corporal bent down under the weight of the body to grab the note and the money.

"Twenty bucks! Some sort of message here, too. What's this Nazi been up to?"

"Shut up and get moving. We've got to get this man to the hospital, now!"

"Yes, sir!"

They carried him down the hill. A small crowd of stunned POWs pulled back as the GIs passed. "Get back to work!" shouted the sergeant. The Germans picked up their saws and hatchets and headed into the trees.

Zuuza. Zuuza. Chop. Chop. Sounds of sawing and chopping mingled with the sharp, whistling wind in the high branches. Molly covered her face and leaned into the raspberry bush, welcoming the painful thorns cutting into her forearms and the backs of her hands. Through the slits in her fingers, she watched Jane approach the bloody ground and bow her head. "God," she whispered. Molly could see her knees shaking under the sagging hem of her dress.

Peter stepped up beside Jane.

"Jesus." He ran his fingers through his hair. "Molly," he whispered. "It's here."

"What's here?"

"Come and see."

Molly straightened her stiff knees, stepped around the bush, and slid behind Peter's back.

"Look," said Peter.

Molly didn't want to look. She'd already noticed the sickening sweet smell of blood. That was enough.

Peter stepped aside, and Molly saw a glint of metal. She dropped to her knees. The watch was half buried in the blood-soaked ground. Molly dug her fingers into the wet earth and pulled out the watch. She closed her eyes, clutched it to her chest, and rocked back and forth, feeling her heart beat strong and steady against the small metal disk.

Her hand felt wet. Sticky. She looked down, surprised to see the German's blood streaked across her knuckles.

She leaped up and ran through the woods, darting right, then left, the raspberry bushes tearing at her pants and sweater as she ran. She heard Peter and Jane trailing behind, but she didn't want to stop, couldn't stop. She had to put distance between herself and that German's blood.

In the shelter of St. George's Ruin, the three huddled around a small fire. Molly pulled her clenched hand from her pocket. The German's blood had seeped under her nails. Red-brown covered her palm, gluing her fingers to the metal watch.

Her stomach turned. She wished it wasn't her hand they were all staring at. She'd never imagined her pale fingers covered with someone else's blood. The blue-eyed German was dying, maybe already dead because of her. And the watch didn't even feel real. It was as weightless as a dime-store toy in her hand.

"Come on, Molly," said Jane.

She tightened her grasp. "I want to look at it alone."

"No way!" said Peter. "Not after what we've been through!"

Molly looked into the fire. She could hear it in Peter's voice. He was blaming her for the POW. For the gunfire and the blood. She didn't want to look at her hand; it was a dirty thing.

Setting her jaw, she peeled back her sticky fingers. The watch lay in her open palm, dirt and blood smeared across the cover. Bloody string where the chain should be. Peter leaned closer. "A letter 'P,' " he said.

"No. It's an 'F,' " said Molly. " 'F,' for Fowler." She looked closer. It was an "F," wasn't it? "It's just a decorative script," she said. "The scratch here along the side makes it look like a 'P.' "

She felt a clutching in her throat as she opened the hunting case. There they were, the Roman numerals, the half-moon. Her father's watch! Biting the tip of her tongue to quiet the shaking in her hand, she turned the watch over and pried open the secret door in back with her fingernail.

Peter and Jane leaned closer. Molly's heart pounded against her rib cage as she stared at the gold disk. Nothing. No piece of folded paper with words of hope. No message at all! She felt the heat of the fire burning the back of her hand. Trembling, she closed the case and paced the rocky ground. "It's not right. I asked him to send me a message if he was in trouble! Now I don't know what happened to him, if he's in hiding, or in a German prison camp. I don't know if he's alive or . . . " She jammed the sticky watch into her pocket. "It doesn't mean anything!"

Jane frowned thoughtfully, "We don't know the whole story. Maybe it was too dangerous to send a note. Maybe all he could do was send the watch."

Molly looked at her friends. They didn't understand. How could they? Peter wasn't close to his dad. Jane had never met her father.

"I wanted . . . " Molly struggled to put it into words. "Something to hang on to." A loon cried as it flew overhead. The sound cut a hollow place inside Molly's chest. Her own heart had slipped down her arm into her hand, wrapped around her father's watch so tight, she could feel the blood pounding in the tips of her fingers.

It was getting dark by the time Molly stood at her back door. She'd left home at three-thirty. Now it was close to six, and she'd have to make up an excuse for being late. She opened the door and stood in the shadow of the kitchen doorway.

"Molly," her mom said nervously. "Glen, I mean, Mr. Henson's here for a visit."

"Hey, Molly." Glen stood up and thrust out his square hand. Molly kept hers jammed in her pocket. She couldn't let go of her dad's watch. Couldn't shake his hand with her bloody one. Wind rushed through the back door, blowing the napkins across the kitchen table.

"Shut the door, Molly, for heaven's sake."

"Sorry." Molly yanked the door shut. "I . . . I . . . gotta go." She bolted through the kitchen and up the narrow stairs to the bathroom.

"Molly! Don't be rude!" called Mom.

"It's all right," she heard Glen say with a laugh.

Facing the mirror, she turned on the tap, grabbed the nailbrush, and scrubbed the blood under her nails till the tips of her fingers stung. "You've got blood on your hands, Molly," she whispered. "Murderer."

eleven

Spies

Sunlight spilled from the dusty window across the steps. Molly gripped the bannister, rubbing her eyes against the morning light as she followed her mom down to the beauty shop. Still half asleep, she took a bottle of ammonia from the utility closet and stumbled toward the mirrors as Mom began to mop the floor. Most of the night Molly had lain shivering in her bed, seeing the German's bloody face, hearing the GI say, "He'll be dead soon . . ." She'd brought extra covers from the hall closet and curled up beneath them, but they hadn't helped. The cold had sunken through her flesh and down into her bones.

Molly sprayed the large, round mirror and tried to avoid her sleepy reflection as she breathed in the familiar smells of ammonia, beauty supplies, and floor cleaner.

Dee Brown strolled into the salon.

"Oh, Dee," said Mom, "I'll be right with you, as soon as I finish with this floor."

"I'm not here for a hairdo today, Gail. I've come to tell you the news."

"What news?" asked Mom, wringing out the mop.

Dee leaned her bulk against the front counter. "A POW was shot while trying to escape yesterday!"

Molly squeezed the damp rag in her hand.

"Are you sure?" asked Mom.

"I got the word from Howard Gross. It'll be in today's paper!"

Molly moved to the next mirror and covered her worried reflection with a soft ammonia mist.

"Did the POW die?" asked Mom.

"No, but he's pretty bad off. He's in the county hospital, surrounded by military police."

Not dead.

Molly wiped the glass, a mixture of terror and relief flooding through her body.

In the wet mirror, Molly could see Mom facing Dee. Dee licked her lips. "All kinds of people want to question him," she said.

Mom leaned her mop against the counter. "What for?"

Dee's eyebrows shot up. "Oh, that's the best part. They have to interrogate him because they found a message written in German. Somebody was trying to help him escape!" said Dee, bunching her lilac scarf in her chubby hands. "Howard thinks there's a spy right here in Keenan! Can you believe it?"

Molly shuddered, dropping her cleaning rag into a box of hairpins. She caught it up again, wiping the glass in a swift circular motion, as if the action would erase her mom and Dee from the room.

"Oh, you and your stories, Dee," said Mom with a wave of her hand. She began mopping again.

"No, Gail, it's true! I swear!"

Mom pushed the mop harder. "There aren't any spies here in Keenan, Dee."

"Oh? Well, there's somebody in town who knows German well enough to write that POW a note!"

Molly could feel her body shaking as she leaned against the door frame. "I finished the mirrors, Mom. Can I go now?"

Mom stepped around the wet spot in the middle of the floor. "You look pale, honey. Are you all right?"

Dee crossed her arms. "She's sick, Gail. Just look at her. She's white as a sheet."

Mom felt Molly's head. "She didn't touch her dinner last night or her breakfast this morning."

"The flu," announced Dee.

Mom ran her hand through Molly's hair. "You'd better go upstairs and get in bed, honey."

Molly grabbed the bannister and dragged herself up the stairs to the kitchen and started up the second flight to her bedroom.

She'd wanted the watch so much. Needed to

know that she was right about her dad. That everyone else was wrong. But she hadn't expected the gunfire, the blood. She hadn't wanted anyone to get hurt.

He's not dead, she reminded herself with every step. The bright light from her bedroom windows hurt her eyes. She drew the blackout curtains, lit a candle, and sat on her bed, watching the flame shudder in rhythm to her swift, hot breaths. After a time, her breaths deepened, and the candle flame grew stronger.

The POW was alive, and that was good, very good. But he was surrounded by MPs. Would they find out about the watch? Molly pulled the little brown box from her desk drawer and curled up on her bed. In the dim light beneath her quilt, she wound the watch and held it to her cheek. Come home, she whispered in rhythm to the small ticking sound. Come home now.

A pebble struck Molly's window. She climbed out of bed and took a deep breath to check her dizziness. She'd lain in bed all day, feigning sleep when Grandma or her mom came in, leaving the food on her tray, untouched.

Lifting the blackout curtain to peer into the twilight, she spotted a shadow stepping out from behind the apple tree. Peter. Molly threw on her clothes and shoes, slipped out her window, and climbed down the scratchy branches, landing on the damp grass with a thud.

"What's up?" she asked.

"It's Mrs. Larkin!" puffed Peter, tugging her around the house toward the sidewalk. "Howard Gross thinks she must have written the note. He and some others are headed for her house."

"Oh, no! When did they leave?"

"Couple minutes ago."

"Come on." They ran across the road, through the alley, and down to the railroad tracks, racing alongside the parallel steel rails till Molly called, "Shortcut!" and dove onto a narrow path cutting through the firs. Molly puffed up the steep path, crashing through ferns and chokeberry bushes.

Breaking free of the woods, they sped up Taylor Avenue to the hilltop and stopped across the street from Jane's house. No light came from the windows, the blackout curtains already drawn against the night.

Molly counted quickly. Eight of them. Frank Dutch. Howard Gross and Earl Peters, all standing in a small clump on Jane's front lawn. Hal Fitzhenry leaned on Jane's picket fence. Pat Brummer to his left, a newspaper rolled in his hand. At the bottom of Jane's steps, Sam, Joe, and Robbie stood whacking at a leafless rosebush with long sticks.

"Come out, May!" shouted Mr. Gross. "We got some talking to do."

No sound from the dark house.

Molly crossed the road, crept through the gate, and wedged herself between Frank Dutch and Mr. Gross.

"Come out," called Mr. Dutch, his breath reeking

of wine. "Or we'll have to force you out!" He stepped on Molly's foot as he tottered forward. She jerked away.

"'Scuse me," he said under his breath, then tipped his head, narrowing his eyes at her as if she were something the garbage man had left behind.

The front door opened a crack.

"Here she comes!" shouted Sam.

Jane poked her head out.

"Wrong one," announced Robbie.

Jane stepped onto the porch, shut the door, and planted herself in front of it. Sam whipped the steps with his stick. Molly felt the cracking sound against her teeth. *Crack!* She bit the inside of her cheek.

"Get back in there, Jap!" shouted Sam. "And bring out the spy!"

Molly pressed her nails into her palms. If Dad were here, he'd stop this. He'd jump onto the porch, tell everyone to go home and leave the Larkins alone. Suddenly Molly was moving past Joe and Robbie, past Sam, and up the crooked steps till she stood beside Jane. "Are you all right?" she puffed.

Jane nodded. They stood shoulder to shoulder, looking down at the people below. She scanned the darkened faces for Peter. Not there. Across the road? No.

Mr. Gross turned on his flashlight and shone it in Molly's face. "You'd best get off that porch," he warned.

Molly squinted into the harsh light. "No," she said, setting her jaw. She could feel the fear on the back of her neck now, gripping like a cold hand against her flesh. All I have to do is stand here, she told herself. Just stand. Suddenly Peter came around the side of the house. He climbed over the porch rail and stood beside Jane. The three of them were together now. The men would have to pass them to get to Grandma Larkin.

"Get outta here, Jap lovers!" warned Sam. "We've got some business to do with the spy!"

Jane grabbed Molly's arm. "Don't let them," she whispered. "Don't let them take her."

"Who says she's a spy?" challenged Peter.

"The note!" called Mr. Gross. "She's the only one in town who knows how to write in German."

A figure appeared, crossed the road, and leaned against the fence. Glen Henson.

Peter cleared his throat and stepped forward. "You sure about that? What if I said I know who wrote it?"

Molly tensed. He wouldn't tell them about her Dad's watch. He couldn't.

"'I would like to buy your pocket watch,'" said Peter. Then he slowly formed the words, *"Ich möchte gerne deine Taschenuhr kaufen."*

The men on the lawn straightened up as if they'd heard a shot fired. Stunned faces peered up at him.

"He's just makin' it up," said Mr. Fitzhenry.

Mr. Gross turned his flashlight on Peter. "Sounds like German to me."

"It . . . it was just for fun," stuttered Peter, shielding his eyes against the light. "I . . . I wanted a souvenir. You know, a war souvenir. So I asked the POW if I could buy his watch. I'd seen it on him the day I went up there with the other kids." He peered down at Sam on the steps below. "Right, Sam?"

"Liar!" shouted Sam. He dropped his stick and flew up the stairs, knocking Peter onto the porch with a crash. They tumbled down the steps, punching and clawing each other. "Break it up!" shouted Mr. Henson as they rolled toward the fence. He limped across the lawn and grabbed Sam's arm.

"I'll get you later, Birmingham!" shouted Sam, shaking himself free from his dad's hold.

"I said enough!" warned Mr. Henson. "Now go on home!"

"But, Dad."

"Now!"

Sam clenched his fists, blood streaked across his knuckles. He spat on the ground by Peter's head, leaped over the sagging fence, and sped down Taylor Avenue with Joe and Robbie close behind.

Molly and Jane came down the steps and knelt beside Peter.

"Come on," said Mr. Gross. Turning his back on the Larkin's house, he shone his flashlight down the empty street. The rest of the men followed in the dark behind the yellow beam, the scraping sound of their shoes growing quieter as they disappeared over the crest of the hill.

Just the three of them now. The three of them, and Glen Henson towering above them, his face a shadow in the dark. "You rich people make me sick," he said to Peter suddenly. "You think war is about money and souvenirs." He leaned closer to Peter, his left eye twitching uncontrollably, the vein in his neck pounding. "Some of us have paid for this war! Paid with our lives or with our limbs! You go after those POWs for souvenirs again and I'll see to it your butt is thrown in jail, rich kid or no. Is that clear?"

"Yes, sir."

Molly looked up at him. She should tell him it was her fault, not Peter's. Glen should be yelling at *her*. He reached out his hand. "Come on, Molly. I'm taking you home."

"I'll stay here."

"No, you won't. You'll come home right now."

She tensed in her crouched position as Glen took her arm. "Let go!" she yelled. "I want to stay."

"You'd better go ahead, Molly," said Peter. "I'll see you tomorrow."

"You and this girl here better stay away from Molly," warned Glen as he tugged Molly to her feet.

"But they're my friends!"

"Not anymore, they're not." Mr. Henson tightened his grip, led Molly through the gate and down the winding road, the puddles on the street catching moonlight as they passed. Molly worked to calm her rage. Who was he to tell her what she could and couldn't do! He wasn't her dad! She wanted to shake him off, run back to Jane and Peter. But she didn't. Mr. Henson had fought in the war and lost a part of his leg in battle. Her mom and dad would expect her to treat him with respect.

At home on the front porch, Molly's mom opened the door a crack and squinted out. "Molly Fowler! What are you doing out here? You're supposed to be sick in bed!"

Glen stepped around the door.

"Oh, Glen," Mom said, swiftly running her fingers through her red hair before opening the door wider. Molly slid inside, hoping Sam's dad would go away.

"She's been with Peter Birmingham and that Larkin girl."

"What? She has the flu. What was she—"

"I know you do the best you can with her, Gail," he said as he stepped closer, his voice lowering to a whisper. "But the girl's getting out of control. She needs more discipline."

Molly spun around and caught the softness in her Mom's face, the fullness in her mouth as she leaned toward Glen. It was the way her mother used to look at Dad.

"Mom! You're in your robe!" said Molly, leaping forward and slamming the door between them.

Mom turned and grabbed her shoulders. "Molly! What's gotten in to you! You march up to your room this minute!"

Mom opened the door again and stepped out onto the dark porch. "Sorry, Glen, you know she's been upset since her father . . . "

Molly rushed up the steps and slammed her bedroom door. Throwing open her closet, she felt her way into the dark corner. Dad's old coat was there. She pulled it around her and closed her eyes.

Glen Henson's image loomed above her in the dark: the vein in his neck pulsing as he shouted at Peter, the pupils of his pale blue eyes growing larger as he looked at Mom. She pressed her eyelids together, trying to shut out his presence. But it only made him clearer. She imagined him downstairs right now, leaning close to her mom's upturned face, her mom's eyelids fluttering like butterfly wings as he whispered in her ear.

Waves of nausea swept up her throat. Her mouth burned. She buried her face in the scratchy wool, trying to catch her father's smell. Fish. Lobster. Pipe tobacco—the smells were almost gone.

twelve

A Gift and a Name

Peter's back was to her when she stepped out of the woods onto level ground at the top of Keenan Cliff. He leaned over a small fire, warming himself beside St. George's ruin. Molly reached into her pocket for the gift she'd brought him. Wind hushed through the fir trees. No sign of Jane. If she hurried, she could give him the gift before Jane arrived.

"Hey," she called softly.

Peter turned. A purple-green mark covered the left side of his face from lip to cheek. His eye was nearly swollen shut.

"Oh, Peter." Molly stepped closer, wishing she could touch his forehead just above his eye. Her fingers tingled with the thought of it. But she kept her hands pocketed.

"I'm okay, Molly. I know my face looks awful, but it was worth it. When my dad saw my black eye, he sat in my room for an hour. Told me about the first time he got a shiner. He actually said he was proud to see I was standing up for myself. Can you believe that?" Peter's swollen face puffed up further in a grin. She'd never seen him so happy.

"And that's not all," said Peter. "Dad promised to take me on his next business trip."

Business trip? How long would he be gone? She willed herself not to ask as he tipped his head back and stared up at the cloudy sky. "I'm gonna fly for the first time," he said. "Can't wait."

"How long will you be gone?" No. She wasn't supposed to ask him that.

"About a week, then Dad will drop me off back at school. Sounds great, doesn't it?"

Molly dug her hand into her pocket, felt the tin angel and the glass. "I . . . I have something for you." She pulled out the stained-glass eye and placed it in his palm.

"Wow," whispered Peter. "Where'd you get this?"

"Right over there." She pointed past the fire to her digging spot beneath the broken wall.

"Did you find any more pieces?"

"Lots more. I dug up a lot of glass."

Peter held the eye up to the cloud-streaked sky. Sunlight lit the fiery iris surrounding the black slit pupil.

"It's the dragon's eye," said Molly, staring at the

ruin where St. George had once fought his dragon. The stones were moss-covered now. And a cold wind was singing through the hollow window. Peter tucked the dragon's eye into his pocket. "Thanks," he said. He stepped closer. Molly's heart raced. Would it hurt his swollen lip if he kissed her now?

"There's something else," he said.

"Yes?" She tilted her head back expectantly.

"It's about the POW."

She opened her eyes. "What?" Her tongue went suddenly dry.

"He's going to be all right."

Molly's breath cut sharply in her throat. "What about the note and the money they found on him?"

"No one's asking about that. Not since I lied about writing the note to get my hands on that war souvenir."

Molly looked into his eyes. She wanted to thank him. Couldn't find the words. He pulled away from her suddenly, calling out, "Hi, Jane."

"What took you so long?" he asked as Jane stepped up to the fire. She crossed her arms, her elbows jutting out of her threadbare sweater. "I wasn't sure if I should come."

"Why?" asked Peter, breaking a small branch across his knee and tossing it into the flames.

"I'm causing trouble for both of you."

The fire crackled as flames curled around the branch. "You got hurt last night trying to keep people from taking my grandma," said Jane. "And when Mr. Henson took Molly home, he said he didn't want her to see me anymore."

"Not just you," said Peter. "Me too."

"Anyway, Glen Henson has no right to order me around," said Molly. "He's not my dad!"

"He might be someday," said Peter. "He's courting your mom, isn't he?"

Molly dug her nails into her palms. "Don't be stupid, Peter! He's not courting anyone!"

Peter held up his hand. "Okay. Okay, Molly. Sorry."

Yellow flames popped and danced in the damp air. Molly could hear the blood pulsing in her ears. She hated Glen Henson. Hated him almost as much as she hated Sam. Mr. Henson had no business barging into her life, telling her who she could and couldn't be friends with.

"It doesn't matter, anyway," said Jane quietly. "It's not just what Mr. Henson thinks. It's what everyone in Keenan thinks. People aren't supposed to associate with me. I'm the enemy." She held her hands out to the fire and shifted her small feet on the damp ground.

"It's because of those stupid rumors," said Molly. "Everyone saying that your dad was Japanese. But if your mom never told your grandparents who your dad was, it can never be proved. You should just ignore the talk."

"Yeah," said Peter. "Just ignore it. We do."

"I can't ignore it," said Jane. "I have a father. He's real even though I've never met him." Across the fire,

Jane was shaking, her sweater hanging half off her shoulder.

A small, sharp pain shot through Molly's chest, like an old splinter dislodging itself under the skin. She wanted to tell Jane that she understood. Jane couldn't let go of her father any more than Molly could. A daughter had to hang on to her dad, no matter what.

The fire popped, shooting up a flurry of red sparks. They burned out as they fell, leaving tiny trails of smoke. Jane knelt, brushed the fir needles aside, and drew two symbols in the earth with a small stick.

"What are those?" asked Molly.

Jane didn't look up. "Japanese letters."

Molly's temples began to pound. She glanced quickly down the trail to see if anyone was coming. Peter stepped around the fire and crooked his neck to get a closer look. "What do the letters mean?"

"They were on a card my father left for me. Nothing else was on it. It's my Japanese name."

"What does it say?" asked Peter.

Jane hesitated, looking at Molly, at Peter.

"Come on. Tell us," said Peter softly.

A squirrel chattered in the trees above. Jane toyed with the stick in her hand, then touched the top of the first character with the tip. "Ai." She pointed to the second. "Ko. The name means 'lovely child.'"

Molly stepped around the fire and put her hand

on Jane's shoulder. Warmth ran up her arm and spread into her chest.

Jane looked up, her eyes like two dark pools fresh with rain.

"Aiko," said Peter.

"Aiko," said Molly.

Slowly Jane stood. Fire flickered gold patterns into her tattered dress as she rose into her name.

"Aiko," said Jane. "Do you hear me, Father? I am Aiko."

The next day after school, Molly met Jane under the willow tree. Hidden by the long green willow tresses, the girls talked about the watch, the POW, Peter. After a while, they leaned against the trunk, letting the silence between them grow as the April wind played through the leaves. Molly twisted her hair around her index finger. "Jane?"

"Yeah?"

"I've always wondered why your mom went all the way to Alaska to work in a cannery when she could have worked in a cannery right here in Maine."

Jane screwed up her face. "I know. Kind of strange, isn't it? Grandma said my mom just wanted to get away."

"Why?"

"I don't know, something about breaking up with her high school boyfriend."

"Oh," said Molly. A bluebird landed on a branch above, fluttering its feathers and calling to its mate.

"Did your mom ever tell you anything about your dad?"

Jane picked at the lichen on the willow trunk. "She never talked about him much, except to say that he was nice, but things wouldn't have worked out between them. She said they were worlds apart."

Worlds apart. Had Jane's mom meant they spoke different languages, were from different cultures, or that their personalities just weren't a good fit? Molly wanted to ask, but she watched the bluebird instead. It hopped from branch to branch, then took off and disappeared over the school roof. Molly buttoned her sweater. She should be getting home. She'd planned to show her mom the watch today, if she could work up the courage.

Jane touched Molly's sleeve. "Molly," she said, her eyebrows tipped with concern. "You haven't . . . told anyone, have you?"

"Told anyone what?"

Jane lowered her voice to a whisper. "About my Japanese name."

"Oh," said Molly. "No. I'll never tell."

"Never tell what?" said a voice from the other side of the branches. Before the girls could run, Sam and Robbie burst through the willow leaves, tackling Jane and Molly.

"Ouch! Stop!" cried Molly as Sam wrenched her arms behind her back. "Let go of me, Sam!"

"Shut up!"

"Stop it, Robbie!" yelled Jane. As Jane struggled

against Robbie, Molly wrestled one arm free and swung it behind her, hitting Sam on the hip. Sam caught it, pressed her arm back into position, and swiftly tied his leather belt around her wrists.

"What are you doing?" cried Molly. She tried to free her hands. The harder she pulled, the tighter the leather got. Sweat dripped down the back of her neck as she struggled against the belt. She leaped forward, trying to bolt. Sam's hand clamped down on her shoulder, gripping her skin like a vise. She imagined her bones crushing like twigs in his hand.

"Get the Jap over here, Robbie!" ordered Sam.

Robbie tugged Jane over, pressing her back to Molly's as Sam belted their wrists together.

"Stop it, Sam!" warned Molly. She peered through the greenery across the playground. Empty. The teachers were still in the building. The kids had all gone home. No one knew what was happening under the willow tree. She kicked Sam in the shin, then tried to pull away. Robbie caught her and held her in place.

"Oooo! She's pretty wild, Robbie," said Sam, rubbing his leg.

"Let us go, jerk!"

"Aw, listen to that, Robbie. The little girl wants us to let her go!"

Sam peeled a gum wrapper and shoved a square of bubble gum in his mouth. Hands behind his back, he paced in front of his prisoners, "Well. Well. Well," he said around his wad of gum. "Looks like we've got a couple of POWs, Robbie." He leaned close to Molly, blew a huge pink bubble, and popped it. "Aw, look, Robbie. I've made a sticky mess." Sam scraped the pink gum off Molly's nose and cheek with his rough fingernail.

Cold anger rose up her spine. She kicked again. "Let us go, Sam! Stop it right now!"

Sam jumped back to save his shin. "Stop what?" he laughed. "We haven't even started with you POWs yet." Sam grabbed a hunk of Molly's hair, then a handful of Jane's, and tugged their heads toward him.

Molly's eyes teared with pain as Sam twisted her hair together with Jane's and tied it into a knot. Robbie's eyes grew wide as Sam spat his wad of gum into their hair and stretched the piece around the knot. "More gum, Robbie," he ordered.

Robbie hesitated. "Sam, I don't know if—"

"Shut up and give me the gum!" With one arm still on the girls, Robbie jammed his hand into his pocket and pulled out a stash of bubble gum.

Molly and Jane struggled desperately as Sam stuffed wad after wad of gum into his mouth.

"Keep a hold on these prisoners, Robbie!"

"Yes, sir."

"You'll get in big trouble for this, Sam," warned Molly.

"Oh, yeah?" said Sam. "I'm soooo scared." He leaned forward, chomping his square jaw up and down so Molly could see the enormous wad of gum rolling around on his tongue. Her stomach churned with the sick-sweet smell. Sam grabbed more hunks of hair, tied the red and black hair together, and spat his gum onto the knots.

"You POWs should be put in an internment camp," he said, working a pink wad into Jane's hair. "You'd love to be surrounded by Japs, wouldn't you, Jane? Maybe you'd find your long-lost daddy there."

"Shut up, Sam!" said Molly.

Far across the playground, Mrs. LaCasse stepped out of the building and headed for the office.

"Mayday!" cried Robbie. Quick as lightning, Sam unfastened his belt, leaped over the fence, and raced down the road with Robbie close behind.

Molly didn't move. She wanted to cry out, but Mrs. LaCasse had already retreated into the office.

"Let's try to face each other," said Jane. They twisted halfway around and started to untie the knots. The gum was still soft but the knots were tight and intricate. They worked together in frustrated silence.

"We'll never get them undone," said Molly, trying to control the angry shaking in her hands.

"We'll have to pull," said Jane. "It's going to hurt."

Holding their hair close to the scalp, they each took a deep breath and started pulling. Molly felt hot needles burning into her scalp as the knots came apart one by one. She reeled back and stared into Jane's tear-stained face. "Are . . . are you okay?"

"Yeah, I'm all right."

Molly held her pounding head. "I'll kill Sam for this!"

"Come on," said Jane. "We'd better get out of here in case they come back."

thirteen

Short Cuts

Taking a secluded path through town, the girls made it safely to Molly's backyard.

"Wait here behind the apple tree," said Molly. "I'll get the scissors." She raced into the house, crept down the steps to the beauty parlor, stood in a dark corner, and listened. Mom was talking to one of her customers outside the shop door. Good. If she hurried, she could sneak in and get the scissors before Mom came back inside.

Tiptoeing through the shop, she grabbed a pair of shears from the counter just as Mom stepped through the door. "Molly, where are you going with my scissors?"

Molly's hand froze on the stainless steel handle. "I . . . I was just . . . "

Mom rushed up behind her. "What have you done to your beautiful hair?" She lifted the gummed wad of red hair above Molly's head. "Chewing gum!" she moaned. "Who did this to you?"

"Some boys at school."

Mom removed the scissors from Molly's sweating hand. "What is going on at this school? I can't believe the teachers would let this kind of thing happen!"

"There's someone else," said Molly quickly. "The boys stuck gum in another girl's hair. She's waiting outside."

Mom crossed her arms, the tip of the scissors protruding from under her elbow. "You'd better go get her."

Molly raced up the stairs and through the kitchen, knocking into a chair as she headed for the backyard. "My mom's going to fix our hair," she announced, grabbing a branch of the apple tree to catch her breath.

Jane hesitated. "Are you sure she wants me in her beauty shop?"

"Of course she does. Don't be stupid."

Jane followed Molly down the narrow stairway and stepped cautiously into the beauty shop. Mom took one look at Jane, drew the curtains, and posted the "closed" sign on the front door. "You'll be my last customers for the day," she announced.

Sudden shame washed up Molly's cheeks. She stared at the floor, afraid to look Jane in the face.

"Sit down, girls," said Mom, unfolding a yellow apron. Molly sat, looking down at her hands, then up at the curlers piled like some kind of alien fruit in the large ceramic bowls. Looking anywhere but into the huge salon mirrors.

"Chin up, Jane." Mom carefully tied the apron around Jane's neck and faced Molly's reflection. "Where were the teachers when this was happening?"

"It was after school, Mom. The boys caught us out behind the willow tree. Mrs. LaCasse was still inside. She didn't see."

Mom held up a clump of Jane's black hair. "Too much gum in here. If it had only been a little I might have been able to get it out with peanut butter, but as it is . . ."

She picked up the scissors and clipped a knot of Jane's hair. "I guess these things do happen," she said, sighing. "When I was in ninth grade a boy stole my sweater. No one believed me when I said he'd taken it. I was furious!"

"What happened?" asked Jane.

Mom singled out a tangled piece of black hair and clipped. "I found the sweater hanging on the back of my chair the next week. There was a flower in the pocket." She snipped at a hunk of gum below Jane's left ear. "A couple of years later that same boy took me on my first date."

"Was it Dad?" asked Molly with a grin.

"No, not your father. It was Glen. Glen Henson." Mom paused, holding the scissors in the air like a bird hanging on the wind. "As a matter of fact, Glen and I might have married right out of high school if I hadn't met your father and fallen in love with him."

Molly closed her eyes and gripped the armrests. Glen Henson? This wasn't real. It couldn't be real.

"Molly?" whispered Jane. Molly opened her eyes and looked over at her friend. Jane's beautiful black hair was cut to just below the ear. Her throat tightened. "Oh, Jane."

Jane struggled to push back the tears as she looked at the mass of black hair on the floor.

"I'm sorry, Jane. There was so much gum, I couldn't . . ." Mom removed Jane's apron and brushed her shoulders with a whisk broom.

Jane stood up. "I . . . I'd better get home now. Grandma will be wondering where I am. Thank you, Mrs. Fowler." She extended her hand. Molly's mom gave her a quick handshake, then stepped back to toss the apron in the laundry. "Look at it this way, Jane," she said. "Your hair will be lots easier to manage now. No more hundred brush strokes at night in front of the mirror."

Jane's lip trembled. She turned and rushed out the door.

"Poor girl," said Mom.

Molly rubbed her wrist along the bruise left by Sam's belt as Mom dunked Jane's scissors into a jar of cleaning solution. Tying a yellow apron around Molly's neck, she fingered one of the pink wads and let out a slow sigh. "Oh, honey."

Molly steeled her back against the soft chair. Her hair had been long since she was four years old. Mom had never cut it short, only trimmed the ends. What would she look like when Mom was done?

Snip. Snip. Snip. Molly felt a small, sharp pain in her chest with every cut. Snip. Snip.

Dad had loved her long hair. He used to wrap it around his finger. "I'm reeling you in, Molly May," he'd say, then he'd give her a kiss on the cheek before letting her go. She watched her hair slowly falling to the floor. Nothing left now for him to wrap around his finger.

Clip. Clip. Another piece of hair floated down, red curls on straight black locks. Molly's. Jane's. Making patterns on the wood.

"I want to know, dear," said Mom as she ran a brush through Molly's short curly hair, "I didn't want to ask while she was here, but . . . " She snipped behind Molly's ear. "Did the boys at school do this to you for sticking up for that Japanese girl?"

"No! I mean they found us together, but—"

"Who? Who found you together, Molly? I want you to tell me."

Molly grabbed a curl and tugged it down to her jawbone. "It was Robbie and . . . " She looked at her mom's concerned reflection. "And Sam."

Mom's back stiffened. "Sam Henson?"

Molly nodded, pulling her hair down harder till her eyes stung. Maybe this would be it, the thing that would make Mom turn the Hensons away from their door. The haircut would be worth it if Mom . . .

"Sam probably has a crush on you, honey."

"A crush!" Molly's flesh went cold. "Sam did this to me because he hates me! He's hated me for years, and he hates Jane!"

"Hush now, Molly. I'm sure he didn't mean to be cruel."

Molly leaped from her chair. "You're just saying that because you like his dad! Well, you can't marry Glen! You can't!"

Mom slapped the brush onto the counter. "No one has said anything about marriage, Molly May!"

Molly stepped back. "Well, that's good, because you can't marry anybody! You're already married!" She was shaking now. The yellow apron hung half off her neck.

"Molly," said Mom, her cheeks going pale. "It's been seven months since we got the news about your dad. I thought by now you'd be . . . " She stepped closer. "I know it's hard to let go, honey, but I thought we straightened this all out when the Reverend Olson came over. You told us then that you understood what happened."

Molly didn't answer. Cold. She felt cold. Mom put her arms around her. "Molly, you know how much I loved your dad. I'd do anything to bring him back! Anything!" She held Molly tighter. "But he's not coming back. Not tomorrow. Not the day after."

Mom's arms felt heavy. "You have to accept the truth. I know it hurts, honey, but we have to move on. Make a new life."

Molly pushed her mom away. "Is that what you're going to do? Make a new life with Glen Henson?"

"What? I don't know . . . I . . . "

Molly tore off her apron and threw it on the floor. "Honey, there's something I have to tell you. The

Hensons are coming over to dinner tomorrow night. I . . . I've already invited them. I can't cancel now."

Molly bolted up the stairs, slammed her bedroom door, and leaned against it. Heart pounding, she closed her eyes, thrust her hand into her pocket, and squeezed Peter's angel tight, tight, till she could feel the wings bending down flat onto the small tin back.

fourteen

Dinner with the Hensons

Molly looked intently into the small square mirror on her closet door. She tucked her short hair behind her ear. It fell into her face again. She wished she could stay in her room for a year, maybe two. Stay inside like a princess in a tower until her hair grew back again. Instead, she'd have to go downstairs in a few hours and sit with the Hensons.

Crossing her room, she tugged the box of stained glass out from under her bed and began sorting the colored glass into piles along the edge of her rug. If only it were this easy to sort through her life. She pulled the half-finished stained-glass window onto her rag rug, and fingered the spine of the headless dragon. She couldn't stop the Hensons from coming to dinner, but she could finish the window today.

A soft wind lifted her white curtain as Molly arranged the green glass into a dragon's head and carefully glued it down. After some trial and error, she chose some tiny red shards to piece together a new dragon's eye. When the head was done, she plucked a piece of yellow glass from the smallest pile. She hadn't found all the pieces of the dragon's fire. The photograph in her library book showed more. But she was making her own dragon. She bit her lip as she glued the yellow glass in place. Now the dragon spewed fire at St. George.

Molly changed positions on the floor and wiped the glue from her fingers. She'd missed her chance to show her mom the watch today. Too many customers and Mom would be in the salon doing Mrs. Fitzhenry's hair up until dinnertime. But, tonight, after the Hensons left, she'd get her mom alone and show her the watch. Then Mom would be in on her secret. She'd tell Glen her husband was alive, that he couldn't come over to visit anymore. Molly smiled, warming to her plan. After tonight, the Hensons would be history.

Gluing the last piece of dragon fire onto the window, Molly began to fill the space above the creature's head with a blue glass sky. She was lost in her task, working with the glass and glue until her back ached and her legs were sore from kneeling.

When at last, the window was done, she curled up on her rug and watched the afternoon sunlight play along the colored glass. Yes, some of the pieces were missing. The dragon was smaller and had a red eye. But the stained-glass window had come together in a rough pattern that looked something like the photo in the book.

In the fading light, she touched St. George's armor. He looked so small holding his spear and shield against the dragon. She tried to wiggle the glass. It held fast. The glue beneath had dried.

"Molly! Hey, Molly! They're here!" Kevin burst into the room banging the door against the corner of her dresser.

Molly shoved the stained-glass window under her bed. "Get out of here!"

"Mom said you have to come down right now to greet the guests." He crossed his arms and leaned against the doorway.

"What are you looking at?" said Molly.

"Haircut makes you look like a boy," he said, then he sprang back into the hall.

Molly jumped up and slammed the door. She leaned against it, listening for the heavy *thunk* of Kevin's sneakers on the stairway before pulling St. George out again. Lifting the stained-glass window carefully by the old wood frame, she placed it on her desk and leaned it against her window, a nearly perfect fit.

Light swept through the glass and spilled blue-green colors into her hands. Molly danced her fingers in the air and touched the rainbow on her desk. Opening the drawer, she pulled out her dad's watch, slipped it into her pocket, and headed downstairs.

Molly pushed the swinging door open and hesitated. Mom, Grandma, and Kevin were crowded around the dining table with Glen and Sam. The only empty chair was wedged between Kevin and Glen.

"Come on in and sit down, honey," said Mom.

Molly clutched the edge of the door. Glen patted the empty chair. "There's plenty of room. Come join us."

Molly sighed and sat down. Mom passed her a steaming bowl of stew.

Sam leaned forward. "Can I please have the bread, Dad?"

The question startled Molly. She'd never heard Sam use the word "please" before.

Glen shifted in his chair. "This stew looks delicious, Gail."

Mom brushed a stray curl away from her eyes.

"Dad, I asked for some bread."

Glen pushed the bread basket across the linen tablecloth.

Molly smoothed her napkin in her lap. What if Dad walked into the room right now? What if he saw Glen sitting next to Mom? She tried to imagine Dad's handsome face. Would he look angry? Or would he just smile, crack a joke, and slide a chair between Mom and Mr. Henson? She'd love to see the look on Glen's face then.

"Cute haircut, Molly," said Glen.

Molly clenched her teeth and stared at Sam, who hid a victory smile behind his glass of milk.

"I'm rather proud of how the haircut turned out,"

blurted Mom nervously. "Why don't you thank Mr. Henson, Molly?"

"What for?"

"He said your haircut is cute." Mom nodded her head up and down as if trying to reel a thank-you out of Molly's mouth.

"I wouldn't have had to get my hair cut if Sa—"

"Molly," interrupted Mom. "Try some of Grandma's delicious bread."

Molly plucked a slice from the basket. If the haircut was forbidden territory, she'd come at the Henson problem from another direction. "Mom?"

"Yes, dear?"

"Have you told Mr. Henson about how Dad got his Silver Star?"

Mom shot a look of surprise at Molly. "Mr. Henson knows about that, dear."

"Shot down five Messerschmitts," said Kevin through a mouth of bread.

"Rescued a B-17 and all the crew from sure death," added Molly. "Then his plane was shot down and he had to bail out over the English—"

"Yeah," said Sam. "Well, my dad got the Bronze Star for pulling his wounded buddies off the battlefield, *and* a Purple Heart for his injuries. Tell 'em how you lost your leg, Dad."

Glen blushed. "We don't need to go into that, son."

Grandma straightened her chair. "I'm sure we can find more pleasant things to talk about over dinner."

Sam cut a wedge of butter and slathered it on his bread. Mom would have scolded Molly for taking so much of the rationed butter, but Mom didn't even seem to notice.

"I've been thinking about what I'd like to do with the store after the war," said Mr. Henson. "Been trying to save a little money." He waved his spoon in the air. "Someday I'm gonna make Henson's Market so modern-looking, you wouldn't even recognize it."

Molly swallowed her stew. The meat went down like shoe leather. Why was he talking about his store like that? Who was he trying to impress?

"I got loads of money," announced Kevin.

Glen's eyebrows shot up. "Really?"

"Well, not yet, but someday my Superman comics will be worth tons, like twenty dollars or something."

"Twenty dollars, huh," Glen said, chuckling.

"Yeah! A whole twenty! Maybe more."

"Well, well," said Glen, "we'll all be rich then."

"Not all of us," corrected Kevin. "Just me."

"Well, good luck, little guy," said Glen, giving Molly's mom a wink.

Molly dutifully finished her stew and pushed her bowl away.

"More?" asked Grandma.

"No thanks."

Sam slurped loudly and looked over at the grown-ups. He was doing his best to get his dad's attention away from Molly's mother. He gulped down his milk and produced an enormous burp.

"That does it," said Mr. Henson, throwing his napkin on the table. "Sam! Say 'excuse me' to our lovely hostess!"

Sam crossed his arms and clamped his mouth shut.

"All right!" said Glen. "If you can't show some manners, you'd better go outside!"

"Great!" shouted Kevin, leaping up to tug Sam's sleeve. "Come on. Let's go, Sam!"

Sam stayed put, his eyes flitting back and forth between his father and the "lovely hostess." "Nothin' to do outside."

"There's plenty to do out there, son. Now go on!"

Sam gripped the edge of the table, the skin beneath his nails turning white. Molly tensed, waiting for him to push the table over and spill the stew and all the dishes onto the dining room floor. But Sam stared at his dad and lowered his hands to his lap, his eyes softening. "Yes, sir," he said. He scraped his chair back and went through the kitchen out the back door with Kevin close at his heels.

"You wanna play baseball?" Kevin asked as the screen door slammed. "I got a bat."

Molly sat, stunned. She'd never seen Sam give in so easily before. Glen lit a cigarette, leaned back, and brushed Mom's hair away from her shoulder. Blowing a gray stream of smoke, he placed his hand on the back of her chair.

"Molly," said Mom. "Why don't you go out with the boys." Molly sat motionless, her eyes on Glen's broad hand.

"Molly," said Glen, "did you hear what your mother said?"

"I heard." Molly marched through the kitchen and headed for the back porch, slamming the screen door behind her. Glen had touched her mom's hair. How dare he touch her like that! She slumped down on the wicker chair. Grandma came out and sat in the rocker beside her. A bluebottle fly buzzed past, landing on the edge of the little wooden table. Molly brushed it away.

"Are you all right, Molly May?"

"No. Glen likes Mom. I think she likes him, too."

Grandma patted Molly's hand. "Well, that's to be expected. Gail's young. She's alone and—"

"She's not alone. She has us!" Molly wanted to say, "She has Dad," too, but she swallowed the words and stared across the yard. Under the apple tree, Sam was helping Kevin hold the bat. Slowly, almost tenderly, he showed him how to swing.

Sam ran across the yard. "Ready?"

"Yep," called Kevin.

Sam pitched. Kevin swung. Missed. Sam ran for the ball and pitched again. Missed.

"Don't worry, Kevin. You'll get it," called Sam. He stood very still, then reared back and tossed the ball. This time Kevin hit hard. *Whack!* The ball flew over the back steps and down to the beach below.

"Race ya!" shouted Kevin. Molly frowned as she watched them run down the stairs after the ball.

"I know it's hard for you, Molly," Grandma was saying. "But you have to try to understand your mother. A grown woman needs a man. And Mr. Henson . . . well, they've known each other for years. I remember when he used to come to call. All dressed up with his hair slicked back. They probably would have gotten married if Gail hadn't met your father."

"I know," Molly said, sighing. "Mom told me."

Grandma stared at her Victory garden. Bean shoots were just beginning to poke up from the soil. "Glen never forgave George for taking your mother away from him. He was so much in love with her. I don't think he ever really stopped loving her."

"Is that why his wife ran away?"

Grandma turned sharply. "Molly, you ask the strangest questions sometimes." She pursed her lips as if she'd eaten something bitter. "Mrs. Henson didn't run away. She moved to another town, that's all."

It didn't matter what Grandma said. Molly knew she was right. Sam's mom had left Keenan four years ago because she knew her husband was still in love with Molly's mother. Even back then, Sam must have sensed it, too, somehow. That's why he'd singled Molly out at school, calling her Carrot Head and Foul Breath.

"Grandma?"

"Yes?" Grandma turned to Molly, a wisp of her hair, fine and white as a dandelion, sticking out of her bun.

Molly hunched over her knees and tugged her socks up. No. She couldn't tell Grandma what she was thinking about Sam. Grandma would just deny it. "Never mind," said Molly. She closed her eyes and listened to the creaking sound of Grandma's rocker on the old wood porch.

A robin hopped into a puddle beside Grandma's Victory garden. It bobbed its head, puppetlike, and began to splash. Grandma put her arm around Molly. "It's going to be a lovely spring."

Molly didn't reply.

"I know you're upset about Mr. Henson, dear," said Grandma, "but you must try to understand. We can't stand in the way of your mother's happiness."

"She won't be happy. Not with him. Mom will never be happy with anyone but Dad."

"I know," whispered Grandma. "But it's been seven months now."

Molly tugged on a loose thread dangling from Grandma's sweater. They sat together on the small porch, watching the sky grow intensely red as the sun set behind the mountains. "You'd better go check on Kevin, honey," said Grandma. "It's getting late to be down on the beach."

"All right." Molly crossed the backyard, stood at the top of the steps, and scanned the cove for Kevin. White-tipped waves crashed on the beach below. "Kevin!" she called.

No answer.

Down the beach she saw a horse and rider. Peter? No, he was leaving with his dad tomorrow and was probably too busy to go riding. Probably Joe Brummer on his old mare. Joe often rode along Keenan Cove this time of day. Salty sea air stung her nostrils as she walked down the stairs to the beach, then headed for the boulders scattered along the shore. Kevin's favorite place. He and Sam were probably climbing there.

At the base of the boulders, she turned toward the sea, slipped her hand in her pocket, and pulled out her dad's watch: 6:10. A wave crashed to shore. Pebbles tumbled seaward as the wave drew back. In the quiet moment before the next wave, she held the watch to her ear. *Tick. Tick. Tick.* The familiar sound like a small heartbeat pleased her.

She should climb the rocks and look for Kevin, but that could wait. For now she had the watch, and the sea was washing up the beach, leaving shells and ribbon kelp. A sand crab scuttled past her feet. She stooped to watch its crazy sideways race and ran her fingers across some glasswort sprouting in the pebbles.

"Who goes there?" called a voice from above.

Molly came to a sudden stand, and shoved the watch into her pocket.

"Hey!" said Sam, peering down from the climbing rocks. "What are you hiding?" He leaped onto the beach behind her, grabbed her arms, and slid his hand into her pocket. "Ooooo! Lookie here!" he said, dangling the watch inches above her eyes. "This wouldn't be the watch Peter swindled from the POW, would it?"

"Give it back, creep!" shouted Molly. She broke free and spun around, grabbing for the watch.

Sam raced back to the rocks and scrambled up the steep side.

"Give it back or else!" yelled Molly.

Sam peered down at her from his perch on the boulder. "Ooooo! You're scarin' me, Fowler." He held the watch out. "Look, there's a hunting case," he shouted. "You suppose there's a spy message inside?" He stuck his thumbnail in the back of the watch and began to pry.

"Leave the watch alone!" shouted Molly. "It's mine!" She gripped the wet boulder, pulled herself up, slipped, and fell backward on the pebbles. Just then, Kevin and Peter rounded the rocks. "Hey!" called Kevin. "Peter was out riding and he stopped to help me find my baseball in the cordgrass."

"Peter," cried Molly, leaping to a stand. "Sam's got the watch!"

Peter looked up along the jagged rocks. "Give it back, Henson!"

"Stay outta this, Birmingham. I'm only teasing her."

Sam held the watch high above his head, waving his arm to and fro like a flagger.

Peter dropped the baseball, found his grip, and scaled the boulders.

"Wait for me," said Molly, grabbing the wet rock and pulling herself up behind him.

"Sam!" Glen called from the stairs above.

Everyone froze.

"Yes, sir?"

"What are you kids doing down there?"

Sam squinted up at his father, who was leaning over the rail high above their heads.

"Just havin' some fun!"

"Well, come on back. It'll be getting dark soon."

"Sure, Dad!"

In the split second it took Glen to turn and disappear back into Molly's yard, Peter scrambled to the top of the boulders and leaped on Sam. The sudden impact knocked the watch from his hand.

"No!" screamed Molly as the watch flew out. She watched it bounce off the jagged rocks and land in the waves below.

"Now look what you did, Birmingham!" yelled Sam. He scrambled down the steep granite face, crushing Molly's fingers with his heel as he leaped down. Then he took off down the beach.

Hand pounding with pain, Molly climbed down and ran for the water.

"Stop!" yelled Peter. "Don't be stupid!"

Plunging into the freezing surf, she stood waist deep, searching frantically for a glint of metal as she fought a retreating wave.

"Come back!" screamed Kevin. "You're not supposed to go in so close to the rocks!"

A second wave knocked her off her feet and sucked her under. Her muscles pulled against the surging water as she swam, not knowing which way was up, which way was down. Panic filled her as she reached what she thought to be the surface, only to find herself clawing at the pebbles. Suddenly two arms surrounded her and pulled her to the top. She sputtered, taking in great gulps of air as Peter dragged her back to shore. "Are you crazy!" he yelled.

Molly lay coughing and gasping on the shore. As another wave retreated, she turned and saw a glint of gold. "There!" she screamed, pointing to her left. "There it is!"

Peter rushed over. "Got it!" he called, surf washing around his legs as he ran back to shore.

They huddled together in the shelter of the rocks. Molly hugged her wet knees to her chest, a terrible biting cold gnawing at her flesh. Peter slipped the watch into her hand. The cover dangled from its hinge like a dry leaf on a spider's web. The glass was smashed. She brought it to her ear. Sounds of crashing waves, her own chattering teeth, but there were no gentle ticking sounds. "Broken," she whispered.

"You can have my baseball," offered Kevin.

"That's okay, Kev."

"I'm sorry," said Peter. "I didn't mean to knock it into the water. I was trying to—"

"I know," said Molly. She closed her fingers around the watch. Cold to the bone. She couldn't stop shaking.

"We'll take it to my dad's store tomorrow afternoon," said Peter. "I'll get Mr. Mossel to fix it." He stood up suddenly. "Well. Gotta go. I left Blaze tied up down the beach."

Molly looked up. "Wait a minute. How can you meet me tomorrow? I thought you were going on a business trip with your dad."

Peter's face hardened. "My dad changed his mind. He's not taking me."

"Oh, I'm sorry. I know you were looking forward to—"

"Told me right in the middle of dinner," said Peter, spitting his words out hard and fast as bullets. "Wouldn't give me a reason. Just changed his mind." He kicked at the pebbles. "I left him sitting there. Couldn't stand to be in the same room with that . . ." He checked himself. "That liar!" He turned and spat in the seaweed, then scaled the rocks. "Tomorrow," he called before disappearing over the boulders.

"Listen, Kev," said Molly as they headed for the stairs. "If Mom asks why I'm wet, just say I was climbing on the rocks and fell into the water. Got that?"

"How come?"

"I want to tell Mom about the watch myself."

"Why?"

"It's Daddy's."

Kevin turned on the step above Molly. His eyes met hers. "Daddy's watch?" he whispered. "Let me see it again."

Molly held out the pocket watch. "There's the moon," said Kevin, touching the glass. He looked at Molly. "The face is broken."

The Vacant Lot

Night wind rattled the windows. Molly sat on her bed in the dim candlelight. The thought of giving Mr. Mossel the watch troubled her. Broken as it was, she wasn't sure she could part with it.

She touched the glass on the face, feeling the jagged lines across her fingertips. The front of the case hung from its twisted hinge. The hands were still. The moon had ceased turning.

She knew she'd waited too long to show her mom the watch. Now it was broken. It may never be right again. Molly closed her eyes, letting the candlelight paint a gold veil across her eyelids. For seven months she'd been the only one in her family who had believed Dad was alive. She'd thought the winter would be the worst of it, the endless snow, day plunging into night by four o'clock. But spring had turned out to be harder. The new, green shoots poking out of the ground, the bluebirds and robins singing in the birch trees, all made her chest burn with the thought of her dad. She was tired of carrying her secret alone.

Slipping on her robe and dropping the watch into the terry cloth pocket, she reached for her candle and tiptoed down the hall. A narrow shaft of light spilled down the edge of the bedroom door. Mom was awake. Holding the candle high, she peered through the crack.

Mom was sitting on the bed, wrapped in one of Dad's old flannel shirts. Her face buried in Dad's fishing hat, she was weeping softly into the wool. Molly clutched the candle tighter.

How many nights had Mom cried this way, holding a pillow or Dad's wool hat to her face so no one else would hear?

Standing in the shadow of the door, Molly tried to still her breathing, a sudden ache in her chest pulling her downward like an anchor. She was already sinking; if she went in, Mom would put her arms around her and pull her all the way under. Molly stepped back. She couldn't risk it. Couldn't let herself cry. To cry was to believe the telegram. To believe that dad hadn't been able to bail out in time, that he really was . . . dead.

Molly crept back down the hall and sat on the edge of her bed, the broken watch still in her pocket.

She sat unmoving, letting the drops of hot wax sting her flesh as they spilled down her fingers.

Thick clouds drifted over the rooftops across the alley from Birmingham's department store. Molly crossed her arms, shifting her weight from one foot to the other as she waited for Peter. Across the alley, Mrs. Lemieux emerged from her back door with a laundry basket and started hanging out the wash. Molly leaned against a slender birch tree and tried to ignore the sour smell coming from the garbage cans behind the store.

Peter came around the corner and headed down the alley. A stiff wind creased his shirt and blew back his hair. "Sorry I'm late," he said, jamming his hands in his pockets.

Molly shrugged. "We could do this another time," she said. She still wasn't sure she was ready to hand over the watch to Mr. Mossel.

"No," said Peter. "I broke the watch. I want to set it right." Passing the garbage cans and opening the back door marked EMPLOYEES ONLY, he ushered Molly into Birmingham's and led her to the men's department.

Mr. Mossel looked up from the glass counter he was washing. "We're just about to close up, Peter," he said.

"Sorry, Mr. Mossel. This won't take a minute."

Mr. Mossel dried the counter and waited. Molly clung to the watch in her pocket.

"Molly's pocket watch is broken," said Peter.

"Family heirloom. She needs it fixed." He nudged Molly. She pulled out the watch and placed it on the glass counter.

Mr. Mossel checked the torn hinge on the cover and touched the broken glass. "Ah," he whispered with lifted brows. "Phases of the moon. Very nice. How was the watch broken?"

Molly gripped the counter, then realized her blunder and swiftly wiped her fingerprints off the newly washed glass with her sleeve. "It was accidently knocked into the water by the rocks. Can you fix it?"

Mr. Mossel opened the double back and pried off the inner cover, exposing the tiny gears. "I can clean it up, replace the hunting case hinge, and the gears, but I'm not sure I can make it work."

"You have to," said Molly urgently. Mr. Mossel's soft brown eyes flashed her a puzzled look.

"It . . . it means a lot to me," she added.

He nodded. "It will cost a pretty penny. I'll have to order some new parts."

"I'll cover it," said Peter. "I was the one who knocked it into the water."

The watch was placed on a worktable cluttered with small tools and a magnifying glass.

"How long before you get the parts?" asked Molly.

Mr. Mossel shrugged. "A couple of weeks, maybe more. You know how slow the mail is these days."

Molly leaned against the counter, reluctant to leave. She wanted to ask him to keep the watch hidden in a drawer. Somewhere. Anywhere. She didn't like her dad's watch being left out in plain view like that. It was like leaving a part of her body on display.

Peter thanked Mr. Mossel, took Molly's arm, and led her back the way they'd come. They wove their way through the racks of men's suits till they reached women's clothes, where Peter stopped. "Uh-oh!" he said. Making an abrupt right, he yanked Molly behind a rack of pink terry cloth robes.

"Let go, Peter. What's the matter with you?"

"Shh! My dad just came in."

A strong smell of Old Spice filled Molly's nose as Mr. Birmingham marched past them and tossed his brown hat on Mr. Mossel's counter. "Have my new paisley ties come in yet?"

"Not yet, sir."

Mr. Birmingham sighed. "I need those new ties for my trip."

"They should be in any day."

"Well, 'any day' isn't good enough, Avram. I'm leaving this evening!"

Mr. Mossel rushed off and returned with a pile of ties. "How about one of these striped ties?" he asked.

"Come on, Avram. You know I've been waiting on the paisleys."

Peter grabbed the metal rack. "Jerk!" he whispered. "Dad loves to see people squirm."

"I'm sorry, sir," said Mr. Mossel, dabbing his forehead with a handkerchief. "I got the order out early, but the mails are impossible these days."

Mr. Birmingham snatched his hat from the counter. "Show me the hats we've got in stock, then," he said, tossing his into the trash. "That one's bitten the dust."

Mr. Mossel suddenly beamed. "Right this way, Mr. Birmingham."

As they headed for the stack of hatboxes, Peter grabbed Molly's hand and led her out the door into the alley.

"Why didn't you want your dad to see you?"

Peter frowned. "He'd ask what we were doing in the store." He turned down the alley. "You wouldn't want me to tell my dad about the watch, would you?"

He crossed the alley. "Come on," he said. "We can't hang around here. My dad might come out this way." Peter squeezed his way through the slats of a sagging wood fence that opened onto a vacant lot between the Lemieuxs' and the Brummers' backyard. Molly ducked between the rotting boards.

"Came here a lot when I was a kid," said Peter, weaving his way through the wild roses and blackberry brambles. He came to a clearing and stepped around a pile of broken bottles and rusty cans. "Used to be a tire swing back here." He batted a tattered rope hanging from a maple tree. Molly didn't have to ask what had happened to the tire. Probably donated in last year's rubber drive. Some of the cars and most of the bicycles in town were tireless due to the war effort. No one could fault the citizens of Keenan, Maine, with a lack of patriotism.

Peter sat on a fallen log beside the maple tree. Molly hesitated and took a seat beside him. She fingered a clump of reindeer moss sprouting from the rotting wood, then jammed her hand in her sweater pocket and found her tin angel and a loose bit of yarn. She was already missing the watch.

"Wait," said Peter. "Hold still."

"What?"

"There's a spider on you."

Molly tensed. "Where?"

"Hold still, I said!" He plucked the spider from her hair and placed it on the ground. It scuttled off to find cover in the long grass.

Peter paused, then touched Molly's hair again, brushing her curls slowly between his fingertips. Molly stayed perfectly still, not looking up for fear he'd stop. She closed her eyes.

"Your hair was pretty when it was long," he said. "Why'd you cut it?"

Molly bit her cheek, anger filling her mouth with a strange, sour taste. "So you think I'm ugly now."

Peter laughed. "I didn't say that."

She jumped up. "You said my hair was pretty when it was long. And now I look like a boy!"

"Didn't say you looked like a boy, either!"

"You didn't say it, but you thought it!"

"How do you know what I think," yelled Peter. "Nobody knows what I think!" He scooped up a rusty can and hurled it into the blackberry thicket. A frightened mouse scurried out, shot past the garbage pile, and dove under the sagging fence.

Both stood facing each other. Breathing hard. Their eyes full of fire. Molly pressed her nails into her palms and worked to calm her breathing. She wanted to say she was sorry. She'd ruined everything. She wanted him to touch her again.

"Hey," said Molly softly.

"Hey," said Peter. "Sorry, Moll. It's not you I'm mad at."

A flock of geese honked as they flew in V formation overhead. Peter looked up. "I was gonna fly this time," he said. "Really fly."

"I didn't want you to go," said Molly. Oh, she hadn't meant to tell him that.

"Why not?"

Molly nudged a broken beer bottle with her shoe. "Planes crash," she said.

"It's a commercial flight, Molly. Safe as can be. Besides," he said, following the geese with his eyes, "you'll have to get used to the idea of me flying. I'm gonna be a pilot." The geese passed over Keenan, cutting through the clouds above the harbor.

Molly wrapped her hand around Peter's angel, taking in the news. A pilot. She should have known. Hadn't he been loaded down with airplane books when they'd met at the library? And hadn't she seen that look before, the one on Peter's face right now as he stared at the clouds? Her dad had looked up just that way, his eyes full of sky, the day he'd given her the watch on Keenan Cliff.

She bit her lip, chasing the fear back down her spine. She didn't want him to be a pilot. Didn't want to lose him to the sky.

A gust of wind blew up from the harbor. On the

wash line next door, two pairs of long johns fluttered in the breeze. Ghosts dancing.

"Molly?"

"Yeah?"

Peter turned. "You think you could write to me when I go back to Stony Brook?"

Molly blushed. "Sure."

Peter tucked a strand of Molly's hair behind her ear. A flush of warmth spread across her cheek. He was so close. Would he kiss her now? She tilted her head expectantly.

"That's good," said Peter, stepping back and shoving his hands in his pockets. "I hardly ever get any letters."

sixteen

America the Beautiful

Molly sat at Jane's kitchen table as Jane searched her refrigerator. It had been a month since Peter had left her standing by the pile of rusty cans, the tattered rope on the maple tree swinging in the breeze. A month, and she still hadn't found the courage to write him.

"Milk?" asked Jane.

"What? Oh, sure, but just a little."

She watched Jane get down two empty jelly jars and fill them with milk. Maybe she'd write Peter when the watch was fixed, *if* it was ever fixed. She drummed the table. Each time she'd gone to Birmingham's, Mr. Mossel had said the same thing: "Sorry, Molly, I'm still waiting on those parts."

Jane laid out the snack. Molly popped a saltine in her mouth, its flavor spread across her tongue. Upstairs, Mrs. Larkin's radio blared

"You want me to ask Grandma to turn it down?" asked Jane.

"That's okay." Molly tapped her feet to the refrain "Keep the home-fires burning." She'd kept a fire burning for her dad all these months he was away. Not in the hearth like the song said, but in her heart. And she hadn't let the flame die.

Muse leaped on the table and sniffed Molly's jar.

"Come on, kitty," said Jane. "Let's get your dish." She took Muse in her arms, kissed her furry head, and left the kitchen. Molly downed her milk and turned her attention to the old leather photo album on the table. She flipped open the cover, expecting to see pictures of Jane when she was small, maybe some photos of Jane's mom, her grandma, and grandpa, but jammed in the front was a pile of newspaper clippings.

The article on top showed a little Japanese girl, five, maybe six, sitting on a pile of luggage at the train station. She was dressed up, shiny black shoes, a pair of white gloves on her tiny hands. Molly pinched the newsprint hard between her fingers. The caption above the photo read, "Moving Day." But this wasn't an ordinary kind of moving day. The little girl's family had been evicted from their home in San Francisco. They were being sent to a Japanese internment camp in Wyoming.

Molly's heart quickened. Had Jane cut out the

article? She fingered through the layers of newsprint. They were all the same. All about Japanese Americans. Her eyes came to rest on a photo of a grocery store. It was boarded up, the word "JAP" painted across the boards. But in the store window, someone else had painted, "I Am An American."

Jane came in with Muse, saw her looking at the clippings, and turned her back suddenly, placing Muse's dish in the corner by the ivy planter. She stayed in a crouched position, shoulders hunched, talking quietly to Muse. Molly closed the album and tore at a split fingernail as Jane crossed the kitchen and sat down. Sensing Jane's eyes on her, she concentrated on her ragged nail, afraid to look up.

"My grandma clips those articles," said Jane. "She's been afraid . . ." She stared at the album, running the flat of her hand along the stained leather. "That someone will come and take me away."

Molly tore off the split piece of nail. She wanted to reassure Jane, say something like, "Don't mind your grandma, she's got a lot of crazy ideas." But she checked herself. Saying that wouldn't make Jane feel any better. Besides, what if Mrs. Larkin were right about this?

Jane pushed the cracker crumbs around on the table, making first a line, then curving it into a circle. "Grandma was already pretty upset," she said. "But then we started getting phone calls."

"What calls?"

"Someone saying they were coming to get me and take me to a camp. Grandma was scared to answer the phone after that. I was scared, too, until I found out it was just a cruel prank." She looked out the window, trying to hide the emotion in her face.

"How did you know it was a prank?"

"He gave himself away." said Jane. "I wasn't sure at first. I think he must have used radio static to make it sound like a bad connection, and he lowered his voice so I wouldn't recognize him."

"Sam?" guessed Molly.

Jane turned and nodded. "But he made a stupid mistake, called me Jane-the-Jap. Not exactly something a federal official would say." She tucked a strand of hair behind her ear. "As soon as I called him by name, he hung up and never called again."

Molly felt white heat sweeping up her chest. She could see Sam, turning the radio knob to pick up some juicy static, picking up the phone, pitching his voice down low to frighten Jane. "Someone should come after Sam and put him in an internment camp," she said.

"Arrest him and throw him in jail," said Jane, warming to the idea.

"Tie his hands behind his back and put gum in his hair," added Molly.

Jane stared out the window, a slow smile crossing her face. "I'd like to see that," she said. A flock of starlings landed in the apple tree by the back fence. "Come on," said Jane, wiping the cracker crumbs onto her plate. "Let's go outside."

The starlings surrendered the tree to them as they approached. Molly lay down in the shade. Grass blew around her face, tickling her ears as she turned her head. "How long ago did it start?"

"What start?"

"The prank calls."

Jane raised her finger, tracing a pattern in the clouds. "Around the time Sam's dad was wounded."

Molly licked the salt from her lips and watched the bees circling the apple blossoms above.

"You wanna know what I think?" said Jane.

"Sure."

"I think he was scared."

"Sam?" said Molly, coming up on her elbow. "Scared of what?"

"You know. His dad was wounded fighting the Japanese in the Philippines. Lost part of his leg in the battle. He was lying in an army hospital halfway across the world and there was nothing Sam could do about it."

"That's no excuse for what he did."

"I know," said Jane.

They lay in the grass a little longer, talking about Sam. About the war. About Peter. Molly had just stood up to brush the grass from her jeans, when the upstairs window flew open. Mrs. Larkin poked her head out. "Jane!" she cried. "Come quickly!"

Jane jumped up. "What is it, Grandma?"

"Hurry!" called Mrs. Larkin, her voice cracking with emotion. They raced up the back steps, colliding into each other as they dove through the back door and ran down the hall.

On the second floor, the radio was still blaring. Molly started up the steps behind Jane. They met Mrs. Larkin halfway up the stairs. "The war," she choked, tears streaming down her cheeks. "The war . . ." She sat down suddenly on the step, a ray of sun haloing her gray head.

Jane knelt down on the step beneath her. "What is it, Grandma? What's happened?"

Mrs. Larkin drew Jane to her. The radio announcer was shouting, "'The war in Europe is over! Victory in Europe! Germany has surrendered!'"

Molly grabbed the bannister, dizzy. The air felt suddenly too thin, as if she were on a mountaintop instead of a stairway. No more blackout curtains, food rations. No more men in the trenches. No more sinking ships, air raids, B-17 bombers, Thunderbolts battling German Messerschmitts. No more POWs. Dad would be set free! Her mind raced. She drank the dusty air in gulps like a climber.

On the step above her, beside the peeling wallpaper, Mrs. Larkin clung to Jane. "It's over," she cried, rocking her back and forth. "They can't take you away from me now."

Everyone was spilling out of their houses into the sunshine as Molly, Jane, and Mrs. Larkin headed down the narrow road toward town. On Main Street, shop doors flung open, and people flooded onto the sidewalks. As they passed Pat's Barber shop, Mr. Brummer rushed out, still in his apron. "We won!" he shouted, bumping into Molly as he threw his arms around Frank Dutch. They hugged and pounded each other on the back.

"Just a minute, Jane," said Molly. She crossed the road and ran up her porch steps. "Mom!" she called, running down the hall to the kitchen. There was dough on the counter, flour scattered across the table, but the kitchen was empty. Molly raced down to the beauty shop. Nothing. She ran back upstairs to Mom's room. Empty. Mom and Grandma must have gone outside like everyone else.

Taking the steps in bounds, she raced back to Main Street, met up with Jane, and followed the crowd now moving in a happy river toward town hall. As they passed the row of houses along Quincy Avenue, doors flew open, and mothers came out clutching babies. Their children ran in circles around them as they poured onto the street.

Halfway up the hill they were joined by the high school marching band, which had left practice midsession to join the celebration. Marching in mismatched clothing, they played a sweet and sour "When the Saints Go Marching In." Drums pounded. Trumpets blared, dogs barked, people shouted. The noise was deafening.

When they reached the town hall lawn, Molly scanned the crowd for her mom's red head. She had to find her, to hold her and tell her it wouldn't be long now.

She saw a group of women laughing and talking near the cherry trees on the edge of the lawn, but Mom wasn't there.

"It's a miracle," said Mr. Mossel, coming up alongside Molly. "Think of all the people our Allies are setting free!" He gazed at the flag fluttering in the breeze above their heads, the red, white, and blue reflecting off his glasses.

Howard Gross ran up to Mr. Mossel. "It's over, Avram!" he shouted. They patted each other on the back and embraced.

Molly moved through the crowd, trying not to step on toes or collide into anyone as she looked for her mom.

Everyone in town seemed to be there, shouting, laughing, crying, tossing confetti. She hadn't seen this many people together in one place since the day her dad had taken her to the county fair years ago. She remembered how she'd felt then, sick from the rides, terrified of all the strange faces. She'd clung to her dad's coat, getting cotton candy smears along his pocket.

Making her way past the flagpole, she passed Sam's grandpa, laughing, pounding Pat Brummer on the back. "I was getting pretty sick of those ration coupons," he was saying. "Made running the store a nightmare!"

She spotted Grandma in the noisy jumble. Still in her apron, her hands were dusted with flour. "Oh, Molly!" she cried, holding her tight. Molly buried her face in Grandma's soft shoulder. Her hair smelled of fresh-baked bread. "We'll be all right now," Grandma said into her ear. "Everything will be all right."

Molly let herself sink into the warmth of Grandma's arms as people shouted and the band played. Dad could come home now. From Holland. Germany. It didn't matter where he was. The war in Europe was over. They'd set the POWs free.

"Have you seen Mom?" shouted Molly above the noisy cheers and whistles.

"Haven't laid my eyes on her since the news!" yelled Grandma.

Suddenly Kevin darted past, grabbed Grandma's apron, and dashed away with it.

"Come back with that, you rascal!" laughed Grandma. Kevin ran in and out of the cherry trees, Grandma's white apron billowing out behind him like a sail. Molly raced after him, caught him beneath the trees, and wrestled him to the ground. "Give it back!" She laughed.

"Make me!" They rolled in the grass. Molly grabbed the apron, pulling Kevin along the ground like a fish on the line. "You seen Mom?" she puffed.

"Nope."

She gave one last yank, freed the apron, and raced toward Grandma with the prize, but Grandma wasn't where she'd left her.

The band beneath the flagpole played "It's a Grand Old Flag." Molly clutched the apron, looking for Grandma's gray head. A warm hand clutched her shoulder. "Grandma?" She spun around suddenly. Dee Brown beamed at her, her hair askew, tears spilling mascara down her cheeks. "Oh, Molly!" she said. "I'm gonna cry! I just can't help it!" She stepped on Molly's toes as she wrapped her arms around her in a tight squeeze. The smell of gardenia toilet water filled Molly's nose. She felt dizzy again, as if she'd just jumped off the swing.

Dee pulled away, shouting above the music, "You should be so proud! It's because of people like your father who died for our freedom. Who gave their lives so that we—"

"No!" shouted Molly. She dropped her grandma's apron on the trampled grass and rushed into the crowd, tripping over Joe's feet, knocking into Robbie's shoulder. "Hey!" shouted Robbie. "Watch where you're going!"

She could still hear Dee Brown calling, "Molly! Molly dear!" as she pressed her way past the flagpole and hid in the shadow of the town hall steps. Head spinning, she gripped the black iron bannister above her shoulder, closed her eyes, and tried to catch her breath.

Her body felt hollow, her skin thin. Dee was wrong. Dad hadn't died for their freedom. He was coming home. Soon, in a week, maybe two. If only she could find her mom here among all these people. She wanted to hold her tight and tell her it wouldn't be long now. They wouldn't have to wait much longer.

The high school band switched to "America the Beautiful." A gust of wind blew across the lawn, bringing with it the scent of fresh-cut grass, sweat, cherry blossoms. Jane came up beside her, singing, "O beautiful for spacious skies, for amber waves of grain . . ."

Threading her arm through Jane's, Molly joined in the song. "For purple mountain majesties above the fruited plain . . ."

Molly's eye roved around the happy crowd. She spotted Sam sitting above them on the town hall steps. Knees bouncing, he opened and closed his pocketknife as he stared across the crowd. "America, America, God shed His grace on thee." Molly gripped the iron bannister on the stair, pulled herself onto her toes, and craned to see what Sam was looking at.

There they were under the cherry tree. Sam's dad. Her mom. Embracing. Mom's head against his shoulder, his hand resting on her neck. A cherry petal drifted down, landing in Mom's hair. Molly clutched the cold, wrought iron bannister, as voices all around her sang, "And crown thy good with brotherhood from sea to shining sea."

seventeen

News

A piece of pink confetti blew across the sidewalk. Molly caught it, held it high above her head, and let it go, watching it spiral up toward the clouds. It had been more than two weeks since V-E Day. The wind had scattered confetti all around Keenan. Red and pink paper landed in the trees, and on the shingled rooftops, like decorations on a cake.

Crossing the street, Molly entered Mr. Mossel's yard and walked down the narrow path between the dipping lilac bushes. The air was sweet with spring smells, roses, marigolds, lilacs, and the sting of fresh-cut grass. Molly breathed them in as she climbed the steps, knocked on Mr. Mossel's door, and waited.

The door swung open. "Ah, Miss Fowler," said Mr. Mossel, his eyes twinkling behind his glasses.

"I came to pick up my watch."

"Yes, yes. I often take my repair jobs home. So little time to work on them during business hours. Come in. I've been expecting you." He stepped into the dining room and removed a bowl of tuna from the table. Two long-haired white cats leaped down after it.

"Excuse the mess," said Mr. Mossel. "I don't usually let Moishe and Rivkah eat on the table like this, but we've been celebrating!"

"Good news?" asked Molly.

"The best! My sister Hannah and her family are safe! I got the telegram yesterday. It seems they were hidden in a basement in Amsterdam for three years. Three years in a basement! Imagine!" he said with glee. "I was so worried they'd been taken to a concentration camp like Belsen or Buchenwald. So many people were."

He lifted a plump cat to his cheek. "But we were lucky, weren't we, Rivkah?"

Mr. Mossel set Rivkah on a stuffed chair and brushed the cat's white fur from his vest. "Hannah has a son about your age. She named him after me. Avram. A fine boy."

"That must have been terrible for him to stay in a basement for so long. I mean, I guess if you're old, it might be all right, but . . ." Molly bit her lip and petted Moishe's long fur. She shouldn't talk about older people that way, but she couldn't imagine someone her age staying in a cramped basement, not being able to go outside, run through the tall grass or climb rocks along the beach.

"But he *had* to hide out, Molly. Thousands and thousands of Jews were rounded up. Sent to the camps and killed." Mr. Mossel shook his head. "Ah, but I shouldn't be telling this to one so young, should I, Rivkah?" He scratched Rivkah under her chin. She purred loudly. "'Why don't you just leave the girl alone,' says Rivkah, 'and get what she came for?' And she's right, too," said Mr. Mossel. He left the room humming to himself.

Molly crossed the room and stared out the window, watching the bees fly lazily from flower to flower. Glen had come over again last week, and things were getting serious. If Dad didn't send word soon . . . Molly crossed her arms and shifted from foot to foot. She knew the mails were glutted, the phone lines jammed, but Mr. Mossel had received a telegram from his sister telling him she and her family were all right. And others were getting good news; she'd heard it on the radio and read all about it in the paper. When would her turn come?

Marigolds, bright as fallen suns, dipped in the breeze outside. Molly's skin pricked. Her hands grew cold and clammy. What if she'd been wrong? All this time. Wrong.

"Here it is," said Mr. Mossel.

Molly turned, startled.

"Ah, you were dreaming," said Mr. Mossel. "Beautiful marigolds, aren't they?"

"Yes," whispered Molly.

"Well, it came out pretty nice," said Mr. Mossel, holding the pocket watch out to her. He'd shined it up. The gold glinted in the afternoon sunlight spilling from the window."

"Oh," said Molly.

"Take a listen," offered Mr. Mossel.

Molly opened the cover and held it to her ear. She closed her eyes. *Tick. Tick. Tick.* The heartbeat was back. "You did it, Mr. Mossel!"

She checked the face again. "Did you fix the moon?"

"Even the moon," said Mr. Mossel. "It's a beauty. Swiss. My brother Yaakov in New York has one just like it."

"What?" Molly stepped back, bumping against the stuffed chair.

"Wonderful little double back," continued Mr. Mossel. "My brother keeps a picture of his wife in there. Of course, his watch has an 'M' engraved on the cover instead of a 'P.'"

"'F,'" said Molly suddenly. "'F,' for Fowler."

"Eh?" said Mr. Mossel with lifted brows. He inspected the cover. "No. A 'P,' I think, Molly."

"'F,'" said Molly louder but with less conviction. Mr. Mossel gave her a puzzled look.

"I . . . I've got to get home," said Molly awkwardly. "My mom's expecting me."

"Of course. Of course." Mr. Mossel waved his hand. "You run along now. We're all square with the bill. Peter took care of it before he left. And don't

167

forget to say hello to your mother for me," called Mr. Mossel as Molly flew out the door and rushed down the garden path.

Her feet pounded against the pavement as she raced up the sidewalk toward home. The watch was fixed now, she should feel happy. It was a sign her dad was coming home, wasn't it? She stopped on the sidewalk, heart pounding. In spite of the sunshine, the watch ticking in her pocket, she had a sudden sense of dread. Something bad was going to happen. She could feel it.

Arriving home, Molly raced up to her room and hid the watch. When it was safe in its box again, lying beside Dad's gold chain, she sat on her bed and worked to swallow down the fear that was welling up inside her. Something had frightened her at Mr. Mossel's, and later as she was coming home. What was it?

Grandma tapped at the bedroom door, "Molly," she called, "have you seen Kevin's baseball mitt?" Molly came into the hall.

"We'll be late for the game if we don't find it in the next five minutes," panted Grandma. She swept Molly into a whirlwind search that ended with the discovery of Kevin's mitt in the bathroom closet.

"Now what the blazes was it doing in there?"

"Don't know," said Kevin, slipping on his glove and pounding it with his right fist.

"Well, come on," said Grandma, "or we'll be late." They rushed downstairs. Grandma kissed Molly before going out the front door. "We'll be back after the guests arrive. Save some goodies for us." The next minute, she was out the door, herding Kevin down the sidewalk toward the ball field.

"What guests?" asked Molly, striding into the kitchen.

"Oh, the Hensons are coming to dinner."

"I don't want them here."

Mom turned and wiped her hands on her apron. "Don't be rude, Molly. Now wash your hands and give me some help with the deviled eggs. They're due here any minute."

Molly jammed her hands under the running water, working the soap into a white lather as her mom peeled the eggs. "You keep asking them over. It's not right."

"There's nothing wrong with it, Molly, I'm"—she swallowed, brushed her forehead with the back of her hand—"I'm a widow now."

"You shouldn't be having men over to our house, Mom. You shouldn't—"

"Molly, don't," choked Mom, her cheeks going white as she dropped bits of shell onto the counter. "I know how much you loved your father, how much I loved him. I'd give anything to bring him back." She gripped the counter, fighting back the tears. "I'm doing my best to accept, to face my life now. If you could only try to understand."

But Molly didn't want to understand. She wanted her mom to turn Glen away from the door. Tell him to go away and never come back. That she'd never marry him. Never.

Mom turned to her. Eyes blue, lip trembling. She took a deep breath. "Will you . . . help me?" Working to control the muscles in her face, Mom got the crackers down from the cabinet and lined them up on the plate. Molly watched her mom's back, her tense-shoulders. A stray red curl fell from her hairpins, shadowing her slender neck. Molly could push her, harder, just a little harder, and her mom would cry. She had the power to do it; just a few more words, and Mom would run up to her room.

Mom looked over her shoulder. "The eggs," she said. "Could you?"

Molly bit her lip, stepped up to the counter, and took an egg. They worked in silence alongside one another, peeling shells, slicing eggs, dropping the hard, round yolks into a bowl until the doorbell rang.

"You'll be all right?" asked Mom, untying her apron.

Molly nodded. Mom hung her apron on the hook and went to the front door.

"Hello, Glen, Sam," Molly heard her saying down the hall. The door slammed. Molly grabbed a fork and mashed the egg yolks against the bottom of the bowl. Sam came in and peered over her shoulder as she dumped relish and a glob of mayonnaise into the bowl.

"Disgusting," he said.

"You don't have to eat any," said Molly, scooping the mush into the center of each egg and placing them in a spiral pattern on the plate. Sam took an egg, licked the yellow mass from the center, and stuck out his tongue.

"Don't be a pig!" said Molly. Sam pressed his nose upward and snorted.

"Pig," said Molly again.

"That's what you get for inviting me to dinner," grunted Sam.

"I didn't invite you to dinner!" said Molly. "My mom did!"

"What's going on in there?" shouted Glen.

"Nothing," called Sam.

"Well, keep it down, then!"

Molly ran the tap and splashed cold water on her face.

She pulled out a towel as Sam began to pace. "Things are really screwed up," he said. "Someone's gotta stop 'em. Someone's gotta do something before it's too late."

"Too late for what?"

"I mean wedding bells. Junk like that," said Sam.

"There's not going to be any wedding."

"Wanna bet?" He stepped back, thrusting his thumb toward the living room. "Just what do you think's going on out there, Fowler?"

Molly tossed the towel on the counter, tiptoed down the hall, and peered through a crack in the door. Mom and Glen were at the window overlooking the flower garden. They were standing close to one another. Too close.

She marched back down the hall. "You're right," she said, "Something has to be done. You get the . . ." She stopped midsentence and looked around. Sam was gone. Molly flew out the back door, checked the yard, and rounded the house just in time to see him barreling down the sidewalk. A block away, he climbed the steps to his house above Henson's Market and went inside. What was he doing running home at a time like this? She bounded up the steps and grabbed the plate of deviled eggs. If Sam wouldn't help, she'd handle this alone.

Tray in hand, she headed down the hall and paused at the living room door to listen. Bits of conversation drifted through the door. "She's been terribly upset," Mom was saying. "We all have, of course, but I'm especially worried about her."

Molly gripped the tray tighter. Mom was talking about her in front of Glen. "Reverend Olson came over a couple of months back," said Mom. "But I don't know if he was able to help her with her . . . " Molly burst through the door and crossed the room. "Deviled eggs?" she asked, thrusting the plate between them.

"Oh," said Glen. "How nice of you, Molly." He waved his hand above the tray, like a magician over a black hat.

The phone rang in the kitchen.

"Molly, could you get that?"

"Can't, Mom. I'm serving our guest."

Mom sighed and went to get the phone. Glen chose a deviled egg and took a bite. As soon as Mom was out the door, Molly put the tray on the coffee table. "Gotta go get the crackers," she said before trailing back down the hall. She had to waylay her mom for just a minute. They needed to talk.

"What?" Molly heard Mom saying as she entered the kitchen. "Too much static. I can't hear you." Mom stiffened. Spun around. "What? Who is this!" Suddenly she slammed the receiver down.

Molly stepped closer. "What is it, Mom?"

Mom took the phone off the hook and leaned against the counter, knocking eggshells on the floor. Her face salt white. "An ugly prank call," choked Mom.

Molly reached to hang up the phone. "No!" ordered Mom. "Leave it off the hook!"

"What did they say?" asked Molly, suddenly frightened.

"Something really cruel and . . ." Molly's mother brought her hand to her mouth. "I think I'm going to be sick." She rushed through the kitchen door and fled up the stairs.

"What's the matter?" asked Glen, coming into the hall.

"My mom's sick," said Molly. Sounds of retching came from the upstairs bathroom.

"Sounds pretty bad," said Glen. "Maybe I'd better go up."

Molly stepped in front of him. "Better not," she said. Glen frowned, looking up the steps.

"She wouldn't want you to see her that way," added Molly.

Glen shifted his weight onto his good foot and lit a cigarette. Molly crossed her arms, breathing in his smoke. Would he never leave?

A moment later, the kitchen screen door slammed.

Sam came down the hall, out of breath, shoes muddy, and found them at the bottom of the stairs.

"Where have you been?" asked Glen.

Sam shoved his hands in his pockets. "Had to run home for something." He pulled out a square of gum and popped it in his mouth. Leaning against the bannister, he eyed Molly and his dad, then peered into the empty living room. "What's up?"

"My mom's sick."

"Yeah?" said Sam, working to contain his smile. "I guess this means we should go home then, Dad. Might be catching." Glen looked upstairs.

"Sam's right," said Molly. "I think you'd better go."

"Want me to ring the doctor for you, Molly?"

"No. I'll do it."

As soon as they were gone, Molly ran up to the bathroom and opened the door. Mom was leaning over the sink, rinsing out her mouth.

Molly took her arm. "Want me to help you to bed?"

Mom nodded. "But what about Glen?"

"He's gone home," said Molly. "I told him you wouldn't want him to see you this way."

Mom patted her face with a damp washcloth. "Come on," said Molly softly, leading her from the bathroom. Dust danced in the shadowy room as Molly helped her mom onto her bed. Mom looked so frail in the gray light. She lay down on her quilt, limp as a rag doll.

"Should I call the doctor?"

Mom shook her head.

"Who was it on the phone?" asked Molly.

Mom closed her eyes. "I told you. A prank call. Some sick person."

"What did they say?"

Mom moaned and turned on her side. "You wouldn't want to know," she said under her breath. "It was horrible. I can't believe anyone could be so cruel."

When Mom was finally asleep, Molly went out back and walked down the wood steps that led to the beach. Sitting on the bottom step, she shoved the tips of her shoes into the pebbles and buried her feet. Mom had refused to talk about the prank call, but it hadn't taken Molly long to piece things together. She knew Sam had called Jane's house, scaring her grandma half to death. He must have run home to try the same trick on her mom.

A seagull flew overhead, dropping a clam onto the rocks by the shore. The gull landed, waddled up to the shell, and tore at the exposed flesh. Molly's head began to ache. She didn't know what Sam had said on the phone. Something mean enough to upset her mom so dinner would be canceled, and he and his dad could go home.

Burying her feet deeper in the pebbles, she picked up a rock at the base of the steps and stared at the barnacles, jutting from the stone like tiny white castles in a miniature kingdom. "Someone's gotta do something . . ." That's what Sam had said in the kitchen. Well, Sam had done something, all right, but the prank call was a stupid idea. Stupid and cruel.

A wave crashed too close to the gull's dinner. The gull took off, landing farther up the beach. Molly tossed the barnacle stone into the cordgrass and rubbed her pounding temples. Someone had to stop the courtship, but Sam wasn't smart enough to do it, and neither was she. The only one who could stop it, really stop it, was Dad, and Dad was . . . Molly brought her knees to her chest, a sick feeling rising up her throat. She didn't know where her dad was. She wasn't even sure he was alive anymore.

Goose bumps raised along her forearms as she rocked back against the step. The thing she'd been afraid of, dreaded for so long, had already happened. It had happened in Holland eight months ago.

Molly put her head on her knees, listening to the sea wash up to the shore. It sounded so far away. "God," she prayed, "If you can hear me . . ."

Shadows

Midnight, an owl awakened Molly. She slipped from her bed and opened her window. A shadow rested on the apple branch below. "Hoo, hoo," the owl cried. Molly closed her eyes and smelled the sharp odor of ragweed mixed with the salty breeze from Keenan Cove. Mom had felt better today. She'd gotten up and gone back to work in the salon. And there hadn't been any more prank calls. Mom had seen to that, insisting that the phone remain off the hook.

"Hoo," the owl called again before taking flight. Molly leaned out her window and watched it skim across the sky toward Keenan Cliff. In the deep of the night everything had turned to shadow: the trees in her backyard, the fence at the far side of the garden;

even her hands, gripping the windowsill, seemed colorless. She closed the window, placed her hands on her desk, and leaned her head against the glass.

In the drawer below her hand, Dad's watch was buried in its box. Molly spread her fingers wide across the hard wood and did not move to take it out. She didn't want to feel the weight of it; to see the gold disk, gone to shadow in the dark, or hear its dry, ticking sound. She turned and was about to crawl back into bed, when a noise downstairs made her pause. Was that the door? She put on her robe and tiptoed partway down the stairs.

A shadowy figure crept down the hall. Molly gripped the bannister, fear filling her with a sudden white heat. She tried to scream, opened her mouth, but no sound came. The figured stopped, a ray of moonlight flooding him. A tall man with a scarred cheek. He turned and looked up. She saw his broad forehead, his strong chin, his smooth right cheek, and, in the moon, his eyes. "Molly?" he choked, holding out his hand.

"Dad?" Molly half ran, half tumbled down the stairs, her heart fluttering like a wild bird loosed from its cage. She threw her arms around him. Her father's arms encircled her and held her tight. "Daddy," she cried into the buttonhole by her cheek.

"My sweet girl," said Dad.

Molly slipped her finger through Dad's buttonhole and buried her face in his coat. Smells of pipe tobacco and sea wind filled her nose. Daddy's smell. Molly felt a breaking in her chest, a wave cresting, crashing on the shore. All the tears she'd swallowed, held back for so long, stung her flesh as they spilled down her cheeks.

She covered her mouth with her hand, trying to hush the sounds of her sobbing.

"It's okay, Molly," said Dad. "It's okay."

A door creaked open upstairs. "Molly?" called Mom from the landing. "What's going on? Are you all right?" She flicked on the light and started down the stairs. "George?" she whispered. With a scream, she stumbled forward, falling into his arms. "My God!" cried Mom. "They said that you were dead!"

Dad held Mom as she wept. "I'm so sorry, Gail," he said, running his fingers through her hair. "All these months. I wanted to write, to tell you I was all right, but I couldn't. It would have endangered everyone in hiding." He kissed her wet cheeks. Held her and Molly close.

Kevin and Grandma spilled out of their rooms, saw the three of them at the bottom of the stairs, and rushed down. Now all of them were in the hall, Kevin screaming, jumping up and down, the rest of them hugging, crying.

The deep ache in Molly's chest lessened as she wept. Wave on wave, coming in sobs, till the waves grew smaller. Dad was here in her arms, and Mom, Grandma, Kevin. In the narrow hall she felt the heaviness of the long wait leaving her, as if she had been weeping stones.

The family huddled close together in the yellow

glow of the hall light, the floor beneath them creaking as they swayed.

"I couldn't get a call out of England," Dad was saying to Mom. "Got back to the States last night, but when I tried to call and let you know I was coming home, we were cut off."

"That was you on the phone last night?" cried Mom.

Molly gulped, like a swimmer coming up for air. The phone call had been from Dad, saying he was alive, and Mom had thought someone was playing a sick joke on her. Why hadn't she seen it? She'd been so wrapped up in herself. So sure it was Sam.

Molly stared at her dad's strong face. His scarred cheek. His head and shoulders washed in light. He was looking down at all of them, drinking in his family, his eyes like a solar eclipse—dark, surrounded with a green-gold fire.

"You have to tell us," Molly said at last, wiping her wet cheeks. "Tell us everything."

The family moved into the living room. Dad built a fire, and they gathered around. Mom and Dad on the couch, Grandma in her rocker, Molly and Kevin on the floor beside the hearth. Molly hugged her knees to her chest, feeling the warmth of the fire spread across her back.

Dad rubbed his eyes with the heels of his hands and sighed. Mom scooted closer, wrapping her arm around his. It was the way they'd always sat on the couch, ever since Molly could remember, Mom leaning against Dad, arms entwined like ivy.

"It must have been terrible for you all, thinking I was dead," said Dad. "I wanted so much to get word out and let you know I was safe, but it would have endangered everyone."

Kevin tugged at a loose thread on his pajamas. "Tell us about the crash," he said.

"Kevin," said Grandma, "give your father a chance to breathe."

"It's okay, Evelyn. Kevin wants to know the whole story from the beginning. Don't you, Kev?"

Kevin nodded enthusiastically. "Did you get the guy who shot you down?"

Dad stared at the fire. The light caught in gold streaks across his hair, and shot shadow lines across his scarred cheek. After a long silence, he shook his head. "I didn't even see the plane that shot me down," he said. "Must have come up from behind. The machine-gun fire tore away some wing and fuselage. My Thunderbolt caught fire. I was losing altitude fast."

"So you bailed out," said Kevin, "and parachuted—"

"I could have bailed out," said Dad, "but my plane was heading straight for a farmhouse. If there were people in there . . ." He leaned forward, his brows furrowing. "I decided to stay with the plane. Cut my engines to try and kill the fire. I managed to get enough control to steer clear of the farmhouse. Made it"—he laughed—"just barely."

"Then you jumped!" said Kevin.

"Too late," said Dad. "I was too low." He closed

his eyes. "My Thunderbolt crashed into the pasture, flew apart. If Mr. Bogaard hadn't rushed out of the farmhouse and freed me from the wreckage before it exploded . . ."

"Was it a big explosion?" asked Kevin, wide-eyed.

"Yep. A big one."

"Boom!" said Kevin.

"Quiet, Kev," said Molly, looking up. "You were hurt in the crash," she said softly, hugging her knees tighter. She'd been afraid to ask about the scars. She needed him to tell her.

Dad touched the whitened streaks on his left cheek. "This wasn't the worst of it," he said. "My leg was broken in two places, three broken ribs, and a collarbone." He laughed uneasily. "I had enough metal and glass in me to start a factory."

Mom ran her fingers through his hair. "I wish I'd been there," she said. "I hate to think of you being in such pain while I . . ." Dad turned and kissed her. Molly's heart pounded, happy. The pine branch in the fire hissed as drops of rosin bled from the wood.

"What happened then?" asked Kevin.

"Kevin," said Grandma, "let your father tell it in his own good time."

Dad looked down at Kevin. "Next, the Dutch farmer, Mr. Bogaard, hid me in an underground shelter, and not a minute too soon, Kev. The Germans were all over the farm within the hour." Mom entwined her pale fingers in Dad's. "They interrogated Mr. Bogaard. He showed them the wreck. Told them he hadn't seen a parachute."

Molly tightened her arms around her shins and put her chin on her knees.

"Underground, two Jewish families were in hiding from the Nazis. One of the women, Mrs. Rosenthal, splinted my leg and bandaged my wounds after the Germans aboveground left. Pretty tense couple of hours, I can tell you."

He ran his hand through his hair, frowning. "It was months and months before I was fully recovered from the wreck. By late winter, we started making plans to smuggle me out of Holland, but Mr. Bogaard was having difficulty getting in touch with the Dutch underground. Might have been different if we hadn't been so close to the German border.

"Escape plans seemed to take forever. We were so isolated. Cut off from the rest of the world. Letters or messages would have been too dangerous. Any loose talk about the presence of the Jews, any tip from an unfriendly neighbor would have brought the Germans down on all of us. Everyone, including, Mr. Bogaard and his family, would have been sent to a concentration camp." He swallowed hard. "Some people caught hiding Jews were sent to the gas chamber."

The fire crackled, Molly's eyes stung, her arms ached, she came to her knees beside her mother and father.

Mom put her hand on her shoulder. "Molly held on," said Mom softly. "From the very beginning. She never quite believed you were dead." Mom turned to Dad and blushed. "I even had her meet with Reverend Olson to help her learn to handle her grief," she admitted.

"Is that true, Molly?" asked Dad. Molly nodded. Dad touched her cheek. "That's my girl."

Kevin and Grandma gathered in. Now they were all together, surrounding Dad on the couch.

A few hours before dawn, they all headed upstairs. While Dad tucked Kevin in bed, Molly propped St. George against her window and took out her dad's watch. Now, wrapped in her bathrobe, Molly waited for the sound of her dad's footsteps in the hall. Sitting cross-legged on her bed, she held her dad's watch to her cheek and closed her eyes, remembering what he'd said that day on Keenan Cliff. "Our time together has to stop for a while," he'd said. "But when I come home, I'll put the chain back on my watch, and we'll start right where we left off."

The watch warmed against her flesh, the metal felt smooth, even where the letter "F" was engraved.

Dad knocked on her door. "Come in," called Molly, leaping to a stand. She thrust her hands in her pockets. Watch in the left pocket, chain in the right. Dad stepped onto the rag rug, the candle spilling yellow light across his shoes. "What was it you wanted to show me, honey?"

Molly trembled. Too excited to choose what to do first. The dragon? The watch?

Dad stepped toward the window. "Where'd you get this?" he asked.

"I made it from the glass I found at St. George's

Ruin. I saw a photo of it in an old library book."

Dad lifted the candle closer. He peered at St. George's face, touched his small shield, then ran his hand along the dragon's glass spine, shaking his head as he did so. "I saw some beautiful stained-glass windows in the churches over in England," said Dad. "This is nice, Molly."

Molly blushed and looked down at her slippered feet, a wave of happiness washing over her. "It's for you," she said. "I was going to give it to you for Christmas, but when you didn't come . . ."

Dad put down the candle, turned, and ruffled her hair. "Brave girl," he whispered. "Now," he said, stretching out his arms, "I think I'd better hit the sack. I'm exhausted."

"Just one more thing," said Molly.

Dad yawned and tipped his head as she reached into her pockets.

She was ready for him to put the chain back on the watch. To start time again. Pulling the chain from her right pocket, the watch from her left, she held them out to her dad.

"You kept the chain," said Dad. He smiled and lifted the watch from her hand. "But where'd you get this?" he asked, pulling out his watch and holding it next to hers. "It looks remarkably like mine."

nineteen

St. George's Dragon

Mom recapped the thermos and placed it in the picnic basket as Molly took her last bite of lemon cake. She brushed the crumbs into the grass and watched Jane and Kevin chase Dad along the crest of the hill. The tail of the dragon kite swam blue-green in the sky above their heads.

"My turn to fly," shouted Kevin, running up behind Dad. Dad pulled away, laughing. "You'll have to catch me first!"

"Get him, Kevin!" called Jane. As they darted past the giant maple and out of sight, Molly lay back, closed her eyes, and listened to the wind in the grass. Peter's letter was in her shirt pocket. She could feel the corner of the stiff envelope rubbing against her collarbone. The letter was a week old, and she'd read it twenty-seven times. Or was it twenty-eight?

They had said their good-byes last month on Keenan Cliff. It had been a windy summer day. Molly hugged her sweater around her as she stood beside Peter, looking down at the waves that washed over the old St. George's cross.

"Did you see the sign on Henson's Market?" asked Peter.

"Yeah." Molly crossed her arms and looked out to sea. Mom had told Dad what had happened while he was gone. He'd taken it pretty well. He and Glen had met, talked, shaken hands. But things had been pretty awkward with the Hensons after that. She was glad they were selling.

"Strange to think of Henson's Market without the Hensons," said Peter. He shifted his weight, a soft wind blowing his dark hair away from his eyes. Molly tried not to look at the curve of his cheek, the strong angle of his chin. She took a breath. Maybe now was the moment to show him. She hoped she'd remember all the things she'd planned to say.

Peter shoved his hands in his pockets and watched a tern take wing over the water. "I won't be going back to Stony Brook this year."

"What?" asked Molly. "Why?"

"Going to military school."

Molly tensed. "Why is your dad sending you there? Doesn't he know how much you'll—"

"It's not my dad, Molly. It's me. It's what I want. Military school is the quickest way to get my wings."

"But you'll hate it!"

"Maybe." Peter raised his arm, cupping the sunlight in his hand. A shadow fell across his forehead. "I have to fly," he said.

Molly bit the inside of her cheek, trying to find the right thing to say. He'd been gone most of the summer. Now he was leaving again. She wanted him to stay and go to high school in Keenan. But the look on his face . . . "You'll make a good pilot," she said at last.

"You think so?" He smiled, not at her, but at the horizon, where the clouds drifted as thin as angel hair above the sea.

Molly watched the surf below crash against the dark cliff rocks. Peter would fly, and she would be left standing here on the edge of Keenan Cliff. Looking up. Looking down. Wingless.

Peter crouched down, picked up a pebble, and tossed it over the cliff. It clattered against the rocks below and fell into the churning water. "How is it?" he said, "having your dad back home, I mean."

"It . . . it's different than I thought it would be." Molly clung to the gift in her pocket. She wanted to tell Peter everything, but the words were anchored down too deep. Dad had changed. She wasn't sure if it was the plane crash, or hiding underground for eight months, but Dad was different. He wasn't easygoing like before.

She stared at the long green strands of seaweed fluttering on the old stone cross. Peter came to a stand and stepped closer. Molly looked up, a sweet warmth filling her chest as she drank in his face. His eyelids were half closed against the sun. Soft rays glinted gold against his black pupils. She kept her hands in her pockets to keep from running her fingers along the curve of his cheekbone where a red glow blushed through his skin.

"Peter?"

"Yeah?"

"Before you go . . ."

She'd practiced what she was going to say to him on the cliff today, but looking at him now, all the words fled. Blushing, she pulled the watch from her pocket and slipped it into his hand.

He looked down at the shining disk. "Your dad's—"

"It's not," interrupted Molly. "It didn't turn out to be. I mean, it's the same kind and everything, but . . . "

Peter narrowed his eyes. "So all that stuff with the watch, translating the note into German, risking our lives to get it from the POW—"

"I was so sure it was Dad's," said Molly. She stepped back and clenched her teeth, working her jaw muscles. Maybe she shouldn't have told him. She felt stupid, ashamed of all the things she'd put him through.

"I thought it was some kind of . . . sign," she said. "Proof that Dad was alive."

Things weren't working out the way she'd planned. She was supposed to give him the watch, thank him for all the things he'd done. He was supposed to smile, take her in his arms and . . .

"It probably is a letter 'P' on the cover," said Peter, running his thumb along the hunting case.

"What? Oh, yeah."

Peter opened the case, tipped his head, and smiled. "Full moon tonight," he said.

"I want you to have it," said Molly suddenly. "You fought so hard to help me get it. I needed the watch so much all those months to help me believe."

Her skin flushed hot-cold.

He ran his hand through her hair. "It wasn't the watch, Molly. It was never the watch. You and your dad have this connection. Something so strong, it kept you believing he was alive when everyone else thought he was dead. There's a strength in that."

He touched her chin, turned her face toward him, and kissed her softly on the lips.

Wind sang through the dry grass above Molly's head. She sat up, and brushed a blade away from her cheek. Peter had touched her, just so, run his fingers through her hair just before he'd kissed her.

Plucking a cream-colored blade, she popped the stem in her mouth and chewed. Sweet and peppery.

Behind her now, she heard someone running down the hill. She turned as Dad raced past her, leaped onto the picnic blanket, and grabbed the last piece of lemon cake.

"George!" said Mom. "That's your second piece! You'll spoil your dinner!" Dad shoved a bite into Mom's mouth. She giggled as she chewed, then kissed him playfully.

"Kevin and Jane want you to take a turn with the kite before we go," said Dad.

"Okay, but I have to hurry. I promised Grandma I'd be back to help her with dinner."

"We'll finish cleaning up, won't we, Molly?"

"Sure."

"All right." Mom headed up the hill, her skirt rippling in the breeze.

Molly knelt down and wrapped Kevin's leftover sandwich in waxed paper. "I wish we didn't have to go back so soon."

"Well, we don't want to disappoint Grandma," said Dad, pulling out his watch.

Molly scooted closer and peered at the tiny black hands on the face. The silver moon on the blue background. She touched the chain she'd kept in her drawer all those months. Dad had put it back on his watch the night he'd come home, just like he'd promised. Time had started for them again.

"Open the back," said Molly. She hadn't asked him to do that since that day on Keenan Cliff two years ago. The day he'd left for the war. Dad turned the watch over and pried the back off.

No note, but there was something there, something unexpected. A photograph. Molly recognized it right away. It was the one Dad had taken of the family the summer day they'd played hide-and-seek here in this field.

He'd snapped the photo of the three of them beneath the giant maple tree.

"When did you put this in?"

191

"Right before I left," said Dad. He frowned, shook his head. "Got me through a lot of rough nights," he said. "I spent hours looking at it in the dim light underground. Mom and her beautiful smile. Kevin in his dirty baseball cap. You giving me a challenging look as if to say, 'I'll win this time. I'll find where you're hiding.'"

"But I didn't," said Molly. "I didn't find you that day."

"But you kept looking, Molly. That's the important thing. I knew you'd keep looking."

Molly felt a tingle running down the backs of her arms, rushing all the way down to her fingers. Dad had needed his watch for all those months as much as she had. Maybe more. She looked at her father, leaned close, and kissed his scarred cheek. She'd expected the scars to feel dry and rough as lizard scales, but they were smooth.

Dad's face eased into a smile. He gave her a hug, then drew back and laughed.

"George," called Mom. "The kite's caught in the tree."

"I'll get it," said Molly. She leaped up and raced through the long grass to the top of the hill, where Mom, Jane, and Kevin stood beneath the maple tree.

"I'm afraid it's too far up," said Mom.

"Let me try," said Molly.

She jumped, grabbing hold of the lowest branch, and pulled herself up. The muscles in her arms and legs worked as she climbed through the fluttering leaves. Near the top, she threw her leg over a branch, pulled herself to a stand, and reached for the string.

"Is the dragon ripped?" called Jane.

"No. But the tail's tangled."

"I'll give the string a tug as soon as it's free!" shouted Dad.

They were all below her now, waiting for her to free the dragon.

Breaking some twigs, she unwrapped the string and gently untangled the green tail.

"Now!"

She opened her hand as Dad raced to the top of the hill. The wind swept up from the sea, rippling Dad's shirt, pulling the kite skyward. As Molly watched it wheel above his head, the sunlight caught the dragon scales and filled them with bright fire.

afterword

Is Molly's story true? Yes and no. The characters, dramatic events, and the town of Keenan, Maine, are fiction. Fiction, by definition, uses invented characters and depicts events that did not happen but *could* have happened. For instance, there were a number of men presumed dead in World War II who later returned home with miraculous stories to tell their families. Some spent the war in hiding; some were unreported POWs. Sadly, some returned home to find their wives remarried.

It's also true that German POWs were brought to New Hampshire and Maine in 1944. They stayed in places like Camp Stark in the White Mountains of New Hampshire. There the POWs felled trees and cut them to pulpwood length for the paper mills. Lack of loggers due to the war and the need to produce more paper led to this unusual situation. If you want to learn more about this, you can read Allen V. Koop's *Stark Decency: German Prisoners of War in a New England Village* (New Hampshire: University Press of New England, 1988).

The story George Fowler tells his family is based on a number of accounts I read concerning pilots shot down over enemy-occupied Holland and France. Some pilots were taken as prisoners; others were fortunate enough to go into hiding and eventually escape with the help of the underground.

Chuck Yeager (the pilot later famed for breaking the sound barrier in 1947) had a dramatic escape in World War II. While serving in the Eighth Air Force, he was shot down over France, evaded capture, and went into hiding. With the help of the underground, Yeager managed to escape into Spain. There he was arrested, but he didn't stay in jail for long. Yeager used the small steel saw in his survival kit to saw through the bars. Once free, he set out for England. You can read more about Chuck Yeager's escape in William R. Van Osdol's *Famous Americans in World War II* (Minnesota: Phalanx Publishing Co., Ltd., 1994); in Timothy R. Gaffney's *Chuck Yeager: First Man to Fly Faster Than Sound* (Chicago: Childrens Press, 1986); and in *Yeager, an Autobiography* (New York: Bantam Books, 1985).

Last, I cannot close without mentioning the heroism of the Dutch people during World War II. Many of them risked their lives every day to hide Jewish families in their homes or workplaces. Even in the isolation of the countryside, Dutch farmers, like the one in my story, hid Jews in cellars, barns, storage huts, and chicken houses. One Dutchman said, "We knew that we simply had to help these people, and that the Lord would watch over us all."*

During the Occupation, Jews weren't allowed to travel, so the underground smuggled them into friendly homes using bakers' carts, farm wagons, and crates. Once in a safe hiding place, their presence was kept secret. Fear of discovery was so great that in one case, a mother and daughter visited each other's homes throughout the Occupation and neither disclosed that she was hiding Jews. You can read more about the brave people who hid Jewish people during World War II in *Anne Frank: The Diary of a Young Girl* (New York: Doubleday & Company, Inc., 1952); in Miep Gies's *Anne Frank Remembered* (New York: Simon & Schuster, 1987); in Corrie ten Boom's *The Hiding Place* (Minneapolis: World Wide Publications, 1971); and in Lois Lowry's *Number the Stars* (New York: Dell Publishing Group, Inc., 1989).

Heroes are ordinary people in extraordinary situations, people who move beyond their own needs to reach out and help others. The world is full of these ordinary heroes. Visit your local library and bookstore to read more about them.

* *World War II: The Resistance* (Time-Life Books, 1979) p.146